MURDER AT THE MANOR

A 1920s cozy mystery

A Tommy & Evelyn Christie Mystery Book 1

CATHERINE COLES

© Catherine Coles, 2020

All Rights Reserved including the right of reproduction in whole or in part in any form.

Inspired Press Limited

www.catherinecoles.com

ISBN: 9798670205856

This is a work of fiction. Names, characters, places and incidents either are the products of the author's imagination or are used fictitiously. Any resemblance to actual persons living or dead, business, companies, events or locales, is entirely coincidental.

Editor – Romy Sommer

Cover Artist – Sally Clements

Murder at the Manor

Downton Abbey crossed with Murder, She Wrote…set in a Yorkshire village!

Evelyn Christie has resigned herself to another long, boring weekend at Hessleham Hall, the home of her husband Tommy's family. However, it turns out to be anything but dull when his uncle, the Earl of Northmoor, is shockingly murdered!
Evelyn must use all of her sleuthing knowledge, gained whilst she was a member of the Police force during the war, to find out who the murderer is before the bungling local police decide the earl was bumped off so Tommy could inherit his title.

If you enjoy the glamour of bygone eras like 1920s Downton Abbey and gently, cozy mysteries set in the English countryside then you will love this new series.

About the Author

Catherine Coles has written stories since the day she could form sentences, she can barely believe that making things up in her head classes as work!!

Catherine lives in the north east of England where she shares her home with her children and two spoiled dogs who have no idea they are not human!

Catherine's Cozy Mysteries

Murder at the Manor

Murder at the Village Fete

Murder in the Churchyard

Catherine's Website

www.catherinecoles.com

Dedication

For anyone who has ever had a dream—
because the importance of having something to
aspire to can never be underestimated

Contents

Chapter One 11

Chapter Two 21

Chapter Three... 30

Chapter Four... 40

Chapter Five.. 48

Chapter Six.. 57

Chapter Seven 66

Chapter Eight.. 76

Chapter Nine 84

Chapter Ten 92

Chapter Eleven 100

Chapter Twelve... 110

Chapter Thirteen 118

Chapter Fourteen 128

Chapter Fifteen... 135

Chapter Sixteen 144

Chapter Seventeen 153

Chapter Eighteen 161

Chapter Nineteen 170

Chapter Twenty 179

Chapter Twenty-One 188

Chapter Twenty-Two 193

Murder at the Village Fete 200

A Note from Catherine Coles 201

Cast of Characters

<u>Main Characters</u>

Tommy Christie	- Hero and former policeman
Evelyn Christie	- Heroine, married to Tommy

<u>The Family</u>

Charles Christie	- The Fifth Earl of Northmoor
Edward Christie	- The Earl of Northmoor's son
Lillian Christie	- Eddie's wife
Lady Emily Christie	- The Earl of Northmoor's aunt

<u>The Guests</u>

Westley Harrison	- The family's solicitor
Jack Partridge	- The estate manager
Oliver Turnbull	- Vicar
Isobel Turnbull	- The vicar's wife
Theodore Mainwaring	- The village doctor
Julia Davenport	- School Headmistress

The Staff

Wilfred Malton	- Butler
Phyllis Chapman	- Housekeeper
Mary O'Connell	- Cook
Walter Davies	- Charles' valet
Frank Douglas	- Eddie's valet & First Footman
Arthur Brown	- Second Footman
Gladys Ferriby	- Lady Emily's lady's maid
Agnes	- Lillian's lady's maid
Doris	- Evelyn's maid
Nora	- Kitchen maid

Villagers

Horace Hamilton	- Evelyn's father
Martha Hamilton	- Evelyn's mother
Millicent Wilder	- Evelyn's sister
Reg Wilder	- Millicent's husband
Ethel	- The Wilder's maid
Geoffrey Beckett	- Villager

Others

Det Inspector Andrews - Police detective

Herbert Davenport   - Julia's father

Albert   - The butcher's boy

Chapter One

North Yorkshire, England – August 1921

"Begging your pardon, Mrs Christie," Doris hissed from the doorway.

Evelyn Christie looked up from the novel she was reading. "Yes? What is it?"

"Dinner gong is in half an hour and..."

"I am not ready for dinner. Goodness, wherever does the time go?" Evelyn put down the book and got to her feet. "Is my hair a terrible mess?"

Doris twisted her mouth but did not answer.

Evelyn knew that look. It was, without a doubt, the look they gave her when walking dogs along the breezy north-east coast did not produce a look acceptable for a lady of a certain class. There was no question that the summer sun would have also painted her cheeks an unseemly pink.

"Perhaps I should have started dressing your hair whilst you were reading," Doris eventually replied, somewhat tactfully.

With a haste that she was also aware was very unbecoming, Evelyn headed for the staircase towards the interminable corridor leading to the room that had been assigned to her and her husband, Tommy, for the duration of their three-day stay at Hessleham Manor.

No sooner had the women entered than the door between her room and that of Tommy's flew open. "Darling..."

Evelyn grimaced as her husband stopped halfway into the room and looked between her, Doris and the dog who had faithfully followed them up the stairs. Tommy was tall, elegant and dressed for dinner. Which only reminded her she was not.

"I'm not ready," she said unnecessarily.

"Will you be long?"

"Not at all." Evelyn assured him, shooting Doris a hopeful look.

"I trust Nancy had an enjoyable stroll?" Tommy raised an eyebrow and the dog sitting faithfully at Evelyn's feet thumped her tail at the mention of her name.

"It was very pleasant, thank you. I am completely certain the distance we walked means my dress will fit perfectly."

Tommy took in his wife's petite, slim figure, gave Doris a long-suffering look, then nodded. "I'll leave you to get ready. See you downstairs?"

"Of course. I shall not be long." Evelyn bit her lip as guilt set in.

Hessleham Hall was the home of her husband's family. As a child, Evelyn was accustomed to sitting down to dinner when her rather eccentric mother remembered she needed to feed her family. Tommy, on the other hand, was raised very differently. His father, Henry, was the fifth and youngest child of the Fourth Earl of Northmoor. Although Henry's household had been much more relaxed than his father's, they nevertheless expected that meals were taken at particular times and a code of behaviour always adhered to.

Evelyn had just about managed to pass muster with Tommy's parents, before Henry's untimely death earlier the previous year to Spanish flu but his uncle, who was the current Earl of Northmoor, had a particular way of looking at Evelyn as though she were some sort of curiosity he wasn't able to work out.

Of course, it hadn't helped that she had taken up working as a police officer during the war. The women in the Christie family did not work, and they certainly did not involve themselves in occupations reserved for men.

The only reason they had accepted Tommy taking paid work before the war was because he was so far down the pecking order in the family hierarchy. Nobody really cared what the fourth in line did so long as he did not disgrace the family.

However, after the death of cousin Billy, who was third in line, during the war and particularly since the passing of Tommy's own father, his employment had become a source of family disapproval. The family expected that Tommy would not go back to work for the police when medically cleared but would start helping his cousin, Eddie, run the family estate.

She really must try harder to fit in with the family, particularly as they were at the house for the earl's traditional annual family get-together, to celebrate the start of the grouse shooting season.

The earl had been gifted six daughters before he received the son he had so desperately wanted. No one seemed to know, or maybe they just did not want to talk about, why his wife had passed away at such an early age, but Evelyn was quite certain it was because being constantly pregnant utterly exhausted her. Seven children and three further pregnancies in twelve years probably did that to a woman.

The earl's daughters and their families had not stayed on for the weekend shooting but had left that morning, leaving the house incredibly quiet. However, the earl had invited guests who would all stay for the weekend.

Doris had Evelyn out of her walking clothes and into something much more suitable for dinner with an earl in no time at all.

"No need for any rouge this evening," Doris commented. "The sea air has put a bloom into your cheeks."

Evelyn sat at her dressing table watching in the mirror as Doris stood behind her attempting to pull a hairbrush through her tousled hair.

"I'm aware of the gossip at the cottage," Evelyn's eyes met Doris's in the mirror. "All of those not so subtle comments about blooming."

"I'm sure I have no idea what you mean, ma'am," Doris stumbled over her words.

"The only little Christies running around our home in the near future will belong to Nancy." Evelyn turned her head to one side, trying to see what Doris was doing to her hair. "I am not ready for children."

"Keep your head still," Doris mumbled through a mouth full of pins. "If you don't mind my saying…"

"Doesn't really matter if I do, does it, Doris?" Evelyn said tartly. "You'll say it, anyway."

Doris moved swiftly on with what was on her mind. "Your Mr Christie will need an heir. Especially if Eddie doesn't produce one soon."

Evelyn was well aware that it would be frowned upon if others were to find out she talked to her maid about such things. However, she had spent the long war years as a new bride with Doris as her only proper company and they had lived more as companions than as lady and maid.

Her sister, Millicent, had married and almost immediately produced three offspring, so she certainly wouldn't understand Evelyn's desire not to have her freedom curtailed by an endless procession of small people.

Regardless of whether she liked it or not, she was the wife of the second eldest Christie male, after Lord Northmoor, and they were living in an era where production of an heir was a very definite duty.

***

Doris worked absolute miracles, as usual, and Evelyn made it downstairs in that very minuscule gap between pre-dinner drinks and being seated for dinner. Charles, the current Earl of Northmoor, gave her a look that told her he believed her behaviour was no better than he had decided it ought to be. Eddie, his son, gave her the supercilious look of a man who knew his place and, better still, was married to a woman who definitely knew hers.

Lillian Christie, no doubt, would have arrived downstairs in plenty of time for pre-dinner drinks. Her blonde hair was perfectly coiffed, her makeup expertly applied, and she wore what Evelyn was certain was the absolute latest style.

She was of a similar age to Evelyn, but in all the years they had known each other they had yet to find a single thing they had in common other than the rather obvious fact they were married to Christie men. That being said, Evelyn was thankful her husband wasn't a bit like Lillian's.

Whilst Eddie was stuffy, self-serving and a downright snob; Tommy was fun, had an affinity for his fellow man and respected every person who was pleasant and polite to him—regardless of their station in life.

At dinner Evelyn found herself seated between Oliver Turnbull, vicar of the nearby St Augustus, and Theodore Mainwaring, the village doctor. Neither man could be relied upon for particularly scintillating conversation but, at the same time, neither was an insufferable bore.

As always, the table was beautifully laid out. The cloth was as white as the fluffy clouds that had chased each other through the summer sky that afternoon, and every piece of cutlery and glassware was precisely positioned.

Malton, the butler, stood imperiously at the side table where bottles of wine that he'd chosen to accompany their food stood ready in perfectly arranged lines. Frank Douglas, the first footman, had moved around the table filling up glasses to prepare for the first course.

"Food here is always top-notch," the vicar commented.

"Wine is consistently excellent," Dr Mainwaring chipped in.

"As is the company." Evelyn smiled brightly, hoping it would be enough to cover both her awkwardness and her lack of sincerity.

She preferred the dinners she shared with Tommy in their little cottage. They tended to eat their evening meal with their plates balanced on a tray as they sat in the armchairs stationed on either side of a roaring fire. Occasionally they would have a glass of wine to accompany their meal, but never did they drink the amount that was on offer at one of these formal dinners.

"It's most lovely to see you again," Oliver Turnbull told Evelyn. "How are your parents?"

"Both well." Evelyn nodded. "Mother is obviously very busy with the dogs. It's the middle of the show season, of course."

What that meant was that her mother travelled all over showing her beloved Gordon Setters whilst her father, now retired, trailed along behind reminding her when it was time to eat and sleep.

A sudden crash caught Evelyn's attention, and she looked away from the vicar toward the earl who had got to his feet and was wobbling, his balance very definitely off, although he clutched the table with both hands.

"Father?" Eddie questioned, but did not rise to assist the older man.

"Drunk again." Evelyn heard someone else murmur, but she wasn't sure where the words came from as embarrassed whispers travelled around the table.

A maid was summoned and made quick work of cleaning up the bottle of wine that the earl had knocked from Frank's grasp.

"Can't a chap be a little off?" The earl let out a guffaw, the word 'off' being pronounced 'orf' as was the case with the very rich, as he looked in consternation at the anxious faces around the table.

Everything always seemed so loud to Evelyn, so forced, so overdone. She, who absolutely was not accustomed to quiet. Anyone who had spent any time at all around a litter of puppies, together with a pack of adult dogs, knew what noise was. However, the strident voices and contrived laughter of Tommy's family always unnerved her. She knew where she was with dogs, their behaviour could almost always be predicted. With humans, however, and especially these people, there was no telling what they would do next.

The earl sat back down, spoke to his aunt, Lady Emily, seated to his right, and picked up his wine glass. Evelyn watched as he took a hefty swig. There was something not quite right. She wasn't sure what it was, but the earl had a look of concern etched on his face that made no sense. He surely had nothing to be worried about.

Charles had spent the last three days with his family. His son was married, and he had a spare heir in Tommy. The war had ended, the terrible Spanish flu epidemic was over, the world was looking a brighter place and especially the earl's little piece of the world.

Both war and the pandemic had caused great suffering to the Christie family. The earl had lost his fourth child, Alice, to Spanish flu as well as his brother Henry, Tommy's father. The war had taken his nephew Billy, just as the Boer War had taken Billy's father, William.

Now, however, his son Eddie had married, ostensibly well, though the only positive thing Evelyn could see in that marriage was that both parties were as fond as each other of living rich, entitled lives as they were self-centred.

Evelyn looked over at Tommy who, she was certain, had also noticed the peculiar way his Uncle Charles was acting. Her husband sat across the wide table from her, meaning conversation with him was not only difficult but also frowned upon in polite company.

She turned back to the vicar, who seemed oblivious to anything being amiss. "Tell me about your adventures during the war, dear, I would love to know more."

Evelyn sucked in the sigh that tried to escape her lips and pasted a neutral expression on her face. "No adventures, vicar. I worked in the police force."

"And that wasn't adventurous?" he pressed. "I should think that made you quite the daredevil."

"Not at all." Evelyn sipped her wine, planning her next words in her mind before she said them out loud. "Women in the police force could not do the same work as men."

"Indeed." Oliver nodded. "Quite rightly so."

The demure and correct response for a lady of a certain class tickled her lips. She twitched them, and pushed it back. "And why is that?"

"Well…" the vicar stammered and looked over at his wife, Isobel, as though she could tell him the correct thing to say. This response to conflict made Evelyn wonder just how often he looked to his wife for guidance. "It's just to say…that…erm…a lady shouldn't have to experience the vagaries of the criminal element of society."

He almost whispered the word 'vagaries' as though he were uttering a particularly offensive swear word.

"I had wanted to help," Evelyn said lamely, wishing she'd just allowed herself to give him the expected response, which was that she herself had joined up only to do her duty and not because she wanted to do any actual sleuthing.

"Very commendable, my dear, very commendable indeed." The vicar patted her hand. "You took your husband's place, of course. Absolutely understandable, under the circumstances."

The circumstances were that she had met Tommy shortly after war had broken out in Europe. She was helping her mother with the dogs and pondering the direction of her life. They had met and fallen head over heels in love, marrying within weeks of their initial meeting. The early years of their marriage were spent apart, with Tommy fighting abroad and Evelyn falling a little more in love with him as she read, and re-read, every word of each letter he sent home.

Somehow, joining the police had initially felt as though she were closer to Tommy, but that romantic notion hadn't lasted long. Tommy had been an actual police officer, Evelyn had not. The local constabulary had allowed women to join them, but they certainly had not been permitted to do anything that seemed very useful to Evelyn.

"Yes, thank you," she agreed weakly.

Now, as they were about to begin dinner, was probably not the correct time to remind the vicar that times were changing. Women were not, for very much longer, going to be restrained by the fact they had been born female. Although she herself was too young to vote, there was now a woman in parliament—whom Evelyn admired so greatly for her pioneering work that she had named her adored dog after her.

Yes, times were definitely changing.

Evelyn was halfway through regretting that here at Hessleham Hall things were very much the same now as they had always been before the war when there came a great shout from the head of the table.

"You, man!" Charles pointed along the table at the village doctor. "I hope you've brought your medical bag with you. There's something terribly wrong with me. I can't feel my ruddy legs!"

Chapter Two

The earl's shocking statement rather put an end to dinner. Some of the men carried Charles from the dining room up to his own room, followed by Dr Mainwaring, who had not looked as calm and reassuring as Evelyn would want her doctor to appear should she suddenly suffer from numbness in her lower body.

The ladies gathered in the drawing room, the meal abandoned, whilst they waited for news of Charles. Evelyn excused herself, ostensibly to check on Tommy though actually because she wanted to know where everyone was, but most of all, to see what they were all doing.

The vicar still sat at the abandoned table, a glass of port in his hand, his empty plate in front of him. Clearly his appetite was not affected by the earl's sudden illness. Though the vicar's girth should have alerted Evelyn to the fact he didn't miss very many meals. Surely, he should be praying. Or ministering. Or whatever it was men of the cloth did when there was serious illness in the vicinity.

The doctor, she presumed, would still be upstairs with the patient. She imagined Eddie would also be with his father, but as she walked past the library, she saw him inside holding what looked like the brandy decanter. She made a mental note to check that out later. Now was not the time to interrupt

Eddie. He wasn't the friendliest human at the best of times, and this evening was a long way from that.

Westley Harrison, the family solicitor, was in the billiard room talking earnestly with Lillian. No doubt the sly cat was finding out how soon she could insist on being called Lady Northmoor, should Charles not survive.

Doris' words earlier that evening came back to her—a horrifyingly clear recollection of every single word the maid had spoken about Eddie's lack of an heir and how the responsibility would fall onto Tommy but, more particularly, *her* ability to produce a male heir should the worst happen. Evelyn suppressed a shudder. How positively hideous to have such a heavy burden of duty.

Where was Tommy?

Of course, the house was enormous. There were many places Tommy could be that she hadn't looked, though she didn't think he'd go too far from the main rooms in case they should need him. Perhaps he had gone for a walk around the garden to clear his thoughts. He did tend to do that when he was pondering a particular issue.

Evelyn made her way back to the drawing room, pausing outside the billiard room, as she wondered whether there was a polite way to let Westley and Lillian know that Eddie was in the next room without making it perfectly obvious that she had been snooping. She gave a decisive shake of her head. It wasn't her concern.

Every head turned her way, wearing expectant looks on their faces, as she walked back into the drawing room. She held up a hand. "I have heard no updates on the condition of Lord Northmoor."

She looked around the faces of those present, not for the first time wondering why on earth the local school headmistress, Julia Davenport, was there. She could understand Jack Partridge, the estate manager, being invited to dinner—that was a tradition the night before shooting season began.

Though, Evelyn now realised, she did not know where he was.

There were no children of school age in the immediate Christie family. Of course, some of Eddie's sisters had children, but Julia had only arrived that afternoon, so her presence made no sense to Evelyn at all.

The vicar's wife, Isobel, who was a nervous-looking thin woman, twisted the material of her rather unflattering beige dress between long, bony fingers.

"G and Ts all around?" Evelyn asked brightly, walking over to the drinks tray.

There was a general murmuring of agreement and some head bobs. She assumed everyone would take a glass. As she began pouring drinks and handing them around, she expected the butler, Malton, to arrive and give her his usual admonishing look. Somehow, she always seemed to do something that he felt the need to chastise her for—never in words. He was way too polite for that, but most definitely with his very disapproving looks. And that was before she started arriving at Hessleham Manor with her dog in tow. He definitely didn't agree with dogs in the house, that was a certainty.

Evelyn ensured Isobel Turnbull got an extra measure of gin. It seemed to her as though the jittery woman needed it though she couldn't begin to guess what had made the vicar's wife so jumpy. Maybe the other woman was simply hopelessly embarrassed that her husband was next door feeding his face when it was very possible the earl was upstairs breathing his last.

Now where had that thought come from?

She poured herself an extra measure. Other than marry Tommy only four weeks after meeting him she'd done nothing that was outrageous or considered out of the norm and so was not given to fanciful thoughts or dramatics like many of her gender—it made the errant thought about the earl's mortality so much more unusual.

Evelyn passed the last of the glasses around the gathered women and took a seat next to Tommy's great aunt Emily.

"I saw you pouring double into old fusspot's glass, so I do hope there's plenty in here," Emily indicated her tumbler. "If my nephew is going to croak it, I want to be prepared."

Usually Evelyn would have murmured something non-committal to Emily and not dared to voice her own thoughts, but it didn't seem the sort of night to leave things unsaid. "And a double G&T will prepare you?"

"I always find," Em said as she leaned closer. "That a stiff drink prepares one for most things that happen in this house."

"In that case," Evelyn told her. "Take my glass."

"You'll learn, dear." Emily nodded, exchanging Evelyn's drink for her own. "It pays to be a little tipsy when dealing with most members of this family. Present company excepted, of course."

Evelyn laughed a little nervously, not sure of the correct response when an elderly lady made it clear she wasn't very keen on the rest of her family. "You have to say that as I'm sitting right next to you."

"Absolutely not," Emily scoffed, raising a quizzical eyebrow. "Surely you know me well enough by now to understand that I am old enough to say exactly what I think and not care one single jot about it. And if I didn't like you, I would most certainly let you know by choosing not to say a word to you other than the obligatory 'nice dress' or 'isn't it fine out today?'."

"Until this very moment, that's about all you have said to me," Evelyn said tartly, recalling Em's weather comment over breakfast just that morning.

"Until this very moment," Emily returned imperiously. "I wasn't sure how much I did like you."

"Um...well...thank you," Evelyn stumbled, not sure what she had done to invoke this new geniality.

Emily waved a hand at her. "Let's not get sentimental about it. Now, tell me, where is that strumpet of Eddie's?"

Evelyn struggled to make the rather large sip of gin and tonic she'd just taken go down the right way and not snort back up and out of her nose in a most unladylike manner. She leaned closer to Emily. "In the billiard room. With Westley Harrison."

Emily nodded. "Of course, she's having an affair with him."

"She is?"

"Most definitely. You only have to watch the two of them together to see that."

Evelyn was about to ask how Emily believed such a thing when Eddie walked into the room, his face showing none of the sombreness he was attempting to project and all the barely contained glee he was clearly feeling.

"I wanted to let you know that, sadly, my father has not recovered. The fifth Earl of Northmoor has passed away."

***

"What was he waiting for?" Tommy asked angrily, walking back towards his bedroom door. He whirled around and marched back to the dresser. "I think he thought everyone would get to their feet and hail him as the sixth Earl of Northmoor and start kissing his feet or something equally ludicrous."

Evelyn opened her mouth to answer as Tommy paused to take a healthy mouthful from the brandy glass he picked up from the dressing table.

"And just as crass." Tommy blustered.

Evelyn waited a moment longer to make sure it was now her turn to talk. "Darling, you do know what he's like."

"I can't pretend I was particularly fond of Uncle Charles, but Eddie was in positively high spirits. It was a bad show, the poor fellow had just died."

"Indeed," Evelyn murmured sympathetically. Tommy didn't seem to need any actual responses from her.

Tommy took another drink before putting his glass down and again treading the same path over to the door. "I don't like to think what this will mean for us."

Panic made Evelyn's heart thump, and she wished she had thought to make herself another drink to bring up to bed. Aunt Em had a point—alcohol was very useful when dealing with the Christie family. "What do you mean?"

"Uncle Charles was at me again earlier not to go back to the force when my leg is healed but to help Eddie with the estate."

Evelyn snorted, all pretence of being ladylike given up in the privacy of their bedroom. "You mean run the estate completely because Eddie will be too busy lording it all over the village and spending his inheritance."

Tommy stopped and frowned at Evelyn, as though he would disagree with her and tell her she had gone too far. He shrugged, then turned his attention to the dog. "Nancy, I fear I will fall over you if you don't stop following me."

"She's keeping you company," Evelyn muttered under her breath. Nancy had faithfully followed every step Tommy took, as though she too was trying to provide a measure of comfort.

"What's that, dear?" Tommy made his way back over to his brandy and finished the amber liquid. "I don't think I'll sleep at all well tonight. There was something very…"

"The brandy!" Evelyn interrupted. "Did you get it from the decanter in the library?"

Tommy turned to face his wife. "Of course."

"And it tastes all right?"

"Well, I thought so." He grimaced. "Now I'm doubting myself. Why would you ask such a question?"

"Did Dr Mainwaring perhaps intimate how Charles died?"

Tommy moved over to the bed and sat next to Evelyn. "Darling? What is the matter? You're beginning to look quite green."

"If what I believe to be true is, in fact, correct, it is you who should look green."

"Now I must insist you tell me immediately what is wrong. You're talking nonsense and that's quite unlike you."

"I do not expect that Charles' was a natural death, was it?"

"Dr Mainwaring didn't say one way or the other." Tommy nodded, as though his thought processes had finally caught up with Evelyn's. "But he said as he left that there were a few things he wanted to check before finalising the death certificate."

"And Eddie allowed him to leave the house after he made a statement like that?"

"Eddie had already gone downstairs before Mainwaring left." Tommy picked up one of Evelyn's hands and held it between both of his. "What is it you believe, darling?"

"Charles suddenly felt ill at dinner. He'd been fine all day." Evelyn held up her other hand and began raising fingers to match the number of points she was making. "His lower body began tingling, then became numb. I've never heard of any illness that starts in such a way and ends a matter of hours later in death. Eddie was doing something earlier on with the brandy decanter in the library…"

"Perhaps he was getting a drink."

"I am not finished. You can pick holes in my ideas when I've finished." Evelyn tugged her other hand free of Tommy's. "I seem to have run out of fingers."

Tommy smiled indulgently. He was well used to his wife's 'little ideas' as she called them and, by now, he really knew better than to try to interrupt her before she finished.

"Now, where was I?" She looked down at her hands. "Oh yes, point six, Dr Mainwaring has left the house without signing the death certificate which tells me he also has some concerns regarding Charles's death."

"Oh, good grief." Tommy stared down at his legs. "And that is why you are worried about me getting my drink from the same decanter Charles used every night before dinner."

"Yes darling." Evelyn pushed him gently off the bed. "I think, perhaps, you should keep up that frustrated pacing."

"How will that help if the brandy has poisoned me?" Tommy grumbled.

"Well, I don't suppose it will," Evelyn agreed. "But it will be very obvious if you begin to lose feeling in your legs."

Tommy ignored his wife's advice and sat down heavily on the bed. He rubbed a hand over his face. "Do you think Eddie was doing something with the decanter or just taking a drink himself?"

"If he was replacing a poisoned decanter with a clean one, then the drink you've taken will be just fine. If he was taking a drink himself, then again we can deduct the brandy is alright to drink."

Tommy nodded. "So, I will not drop down dead at any moment?"

"I jolly well hope not!" Evelyn reached over and planted a kiss on Tommy's cheek. "I rather like you."

"And I rather like you, too." Tommy replied. "Even though I believe you to be an evil little minx for allowing me to think the brandy had poisoned me."

"You do think it is possible Charles was poisoned, though?" Evelyn shuddered. "By someone who could still be in the house as we speak?"

"Yes, I think there may be something to your little idea. It was rather sudden. But there's nothing more we can do this evening. We must wait and see what Dr Mainwaring says when he comes back tomorrow."

Chapter Three

Breakfast the next morning was a sombre affair.

Everyone who had been present the evening before, except for Jack Partridge, the estate manager, was sitting at the vast table eating their way through the mountains of food the kitchen staff had prepared. As they had not got their dinner the evening before, they had prepared extra that morning.

Evelyn, not usually a big eater in a morning, stabbed her third sausage and prayed there would be enough of the cook's fluffy scrambled eggs left for her to have a second helping.

Predictably, Eddie had taken his father's seat at the head of the table and showed no discernible sorrow for losing his father.

Malton, the butler returned to the dining room with a telegram sitting elegantly on a silver plate. Evelyn had trouble chewing and swallowing down her food. Telegrams at breakfast were never the source of good news, and after the conversation she and Tommy had the previous evening, she expected the morning to bring some confirmation of their fears that Charles had been deliberately killed.

Even now, her brain shied away from thinking the word…murder.

There, now, she'd allowed herself to accept what had happened and attribute that particularly grim explanation to last night's events.

With slow precision, Eddie made a grand show of opening the telegram. He was not a meticulous person, so there was no doubt that his lack of haste was being deliberately put on to ensure every single person was looking at him waiting to hear what the missive said.

Once he was certain he was the centre of attention and everyone was focused on him, Eddie cleared his throat. "This is a telegram from Dr Mainwaring."

"Goodness," Isobel Turnbull gasped.

Evelyn frowned in surprise at the woman's over-reaction. The vicar's wife couldn't have sounded more shocked than if Eddie announced the telegram was from the king himself. Who had she been expecting it to be from?

"It says he believes my father, the fifth Earl of Northmoor..."

"Was poisoned." Aunt Em interrupted, finishing Eddie's sentence.

"Really, Aunt Em," Eddie spluttered, furious that she had got there before him.

One of Isobel's hands shot up to cover her mouth, though her gasp was so loud her fingers did not stifle it one bit. She really was acting very strangely. Evelyn added finding out more about the vicar's wife to her list of to-do items.

"Dr Mainwaring instructs that he has been in conversation with the police and we are all to remain in the house and not leave. They are sending someone to speak to us."

"How exciting!" Em remarked. "I hope they send a particularly dashing young police inspector."

"Really!" Lillian said in a voice so scathing it could peel paint.

"I think your remarks are most inappropriate, aunt." Eddie made a slightly more polite effort to rebuke his aunt than his wife, though his bright red face showed he was ready to burst.

"I'm sure," Em retorted. "However, your father could not censor my words in his lifetime and I don't believe you will have any greater success during yours."

Evelyn glanced at Tommy, who was diligently eating his breakfast without looking to the left or right. She knew him well enough to know that he dare not look away from his meal and catch anyone's eye lest he give in to an overwhelming urge to laugh.

The atmosphere around the table positively fizzed, like a newly opened bottle of champagne. Evelyn was now able, after her conversation with Emily the evening before, to see what the older woman meant about Lillian and Westley as, throughout the meal, her sister-in-law sent surreptitious glances towards the handsome and debonair solicitor.

"I wonder who they'll send," Tommy said to no one in particular.

"Do you think you will know the detective?" Evelyn asked.

"Protocol would suggest they will want to send somebody not known to me," Tommy mused. "Though North Yorkshire doesn't have a particularly large CID department, so they may just have to send whoever is available."

"Why can you not just investigate?" Lillian stared down the table at Tommy. "After all, you are family, and you would have this case closed in a jiffy."

"That's not really how investigations work." Tommy took a breath before carrying on. "A very serious crime has taken place. Whoever investigates it will have to do a very thorough job. Not only has Uncle Charles lost his life, but he has done so at the hand of either a family member or a trusted friend. Someone was able to get close enough to Charles to poison either his food or drink. Finding out who that person is will not be easy."

"I would imagine," Lillian said, her voice high and trilling as she made a concerted effort to pronounce all of her vowels correctly. "That if it were Charles's food or drink that has been tampered with, it is quite obviously a member of the staff who has brought about this terrible event."

Emily laughed, laid down her knife and fork and placed her napkin on the table in front of her. "For goodness sake, what reason would a member of the household staff have for killing Charles?"

Evelyn looked towards Frank Douglas, the first footman. How embarrassing that the family were discussing the possibility of a staff member being guilty of a crime in front of him. And who, exactly, did Lillian think she was by suggesting that because something unpleasant had occurred, it must be the staff's fault.

"I have no idea," Lillian said haughtily. "I just know it couldn't possibly be one of us. We're ladies and gentlemen."

"It's probably not a good idea for us to speculate at this time," Tommy said. "The police will be here before long and they will want to speak to all of us individually to find out what we may know. Until that time, it's probably best that we all find something to do to occupy our time before they arrive."

Evelyn could walk Nancy and finish the book she was reading the previous day to fill the hours. She wondered what Lillian did with her time. It was usual for a woman of her position to busy herself with local charities and other 'good works', but as far as Evelyn was aware, Lillian spent most of her time shopping and complaining.

Everyone in the house knew Lillian used her position to get exactly what she wanted when she wanted and didn't consider one little bit the smooth running of the household.

"Should we let someone know where we will be?" The vicar asked, looking at Tommy.

"Yes, I think everyone should," Eddie said, staring venomously at Oliver, clearly furious the vicar was assuming Tommy would have the answer to his question, and not himself.

"No, just so long as no one leaves the grounds," Tommy said at exactly the same time.

"Goodness," Emily commented. "Which is it to be?"

"I am the sixth Earl of Northmoor," Eddie said, entitlement ringing in each word. "Therefore, everyone must report to me where they will be when they leave the dining room and I will pass that information to the police when they arrive."

Emily got up from the table and walked towards the door.

"Aunt Em, where are you going?"

Lady Emily kept walking and did not turn back to look at Eddie.

"Aunt Emily!" Eddie spluttered. "Come back here this instant! You must tell me where you will be."

Emily's only answer was to close the door resoundingly behind her.

"Harrison," Eddie barked. "Ensure every single person in this room tells you where they are going to be and keep a record for me, man."

Evelyn looked across the table at Tommy, who shrugged in response. It was no good arguing with Eddie. He clearly believed that his new title meant that he was in charge. Things would be different when the police arrived, he would learn that it would not matter what his station in life, the detectives would only be interested in finding out who had killed Charles.

***

By lunchtime, there was still no sign of the police. Eddie had announced, as luncheon had drawn to a close, that there would be a reading of Charles's will in the library directly thereafter.

Westley Harrison stood near the fireplace, with everyone else sitting in chairs and sofas facing him in a horseshoe formation.

"I propose to go through only those clauses that are beneficial. All the standard clauses, I shall therefore skip." Westley looked at the gathered group as though he had just said something earth-shattering and was expecting some sort of response. He gathered himself and moved on. "To my Aunt Emily, I leave the ruby and onyx necklace worn by my mother on the occasion of her engagement to my father together with the garnet and diamond five stone ring."

"Both items owned by my mother and loaned to Charles's mother so therefore they already belong to me," Emily muttered.

"To each of my six daughters, I leave the sum of ten thousand pounds." This drew a gasp of shock from Isobel. No doubt it seemed an excessively enormous sum of money to a vicar's wife. There was no doubt that, in ordinary circumstances, no one should be present other than family. However, these were far from normal times.

"This will is old," Eddie said loudly, looking around as though he expected somebody to disagree with him.

Westley looked rather put out that Eddie had interrupted his flow. "Obviously there are subsidiary clauses that take into account what happens to each bequest, should the person receiving a legacy have predeceased the testator."

"That does not change the fact that this is an old will." Eddie got to his feet and moved towards Westley. "This will was made before my sister Alice died. I understood that Father had made a recent will."

Westley did not bother to hide his sigh of irritation. "This is the most recent will and testament made by Charles Edward Christie, I can assure you. If I may continue?"

"Please do." Lillian's voice matched the bored look on her face.

"To my sister, Victoria, the sum of five thousand pounds." Westley paused. "Charles includes with this bequest a paragraph repeating what his father had stated in his will, in that he hopes that Victoria will come home and spend her remaining years with her family. If not at the manor, then at least in one of the cottages owned by the estate."

"Where is Aunt Victoria?" Evelyn whispered.

"Abroad." Tommy shrugged. "I believe she may have married someone the family did not approve of."

"To my brother Henry," Westley paused. "Of course, this bequest will pass equally to Henry's children."

Tommy nodded his understanding. The will was executed before the death of his father and therefore Henry's inheritance would be shared equally between Tommy, his sisters Constance and Grace, and his brother Henry who was known to the family as Harry.

"The sum of five thousand pounds."

"Hurry up, man." Eddie motioned to Westley as he moved even closer to the solicitor.

"And to my son, Edward, I leave my residuary estate…"

"Well, really!" Lillian exclaimed, got to her feet and flounced out of the room.

"Lillian, dear," Eddie called. "Please remember that we must all stay together."

In much the same way as Aunt Em had ignored Eddie earlier that day, Lillian did not return to the room, and neither did she turn around to acknowledge she had heard her husband's words. Clearly, Lillian had been expecting something from Charles that was not contained within the will.

Westley's face creased into a frown as he stared at the door through which Lillian had just exited. Evelyn remembered what Aunt Em had said regarding the relationship between those two. She glanced at the older woman, who sat with her hands folded in her lap, a slight smile on her lips. She inclined her head at Evelyn as though to confirm that it proved her suspicions correct.

Westley struggled to regain his composure, removed a pristine white handkerchief with an unnecessary flourish and used it to dab at his forehead. Evelyn was utterly convinced this was nothing but theatrics. The room was not overly warm and there was absolutely no need for the solicitor to feel under undue stress and therefore have a sweaty forehead. She must speak to him at the very earliest convenience and find out what she could about his personal life.

"It obviously gives the residuary estate to Eddie, which includes all titles and property." Westley continued. "The only other thing of any note is that Charles reiterates that the rule of primogeniture is followed in this will and added a codicil to state that should any person be convicted of a criminal offence they forfeit the right to inherit."

Eddie's smug smile fell from his face, and he swung around to face Westley. "What? What is that?"

"A standard clause." Westley nodded. "The firstborn legitimate male heir shall inherit…"

"I understand that part," Eddie said in a frustrated voice. "Of course, that is me. But what is the other bit?"

"Basically," Westley explained. "Charles added a clause that states, in broad language, that if someone inherits because of criminal means they will forfeit their inheritance and it will pass to the next in line."

"It means, Eddie dear," Aunt Em said, without attempting to hide her mirth. "That if the police prove that you killed your father, the estate will pass to Tommy."

"I will not listen to another one of your insolent comments!" Eddie raged.

"What will you do?" Em asked calmly. "Send me to my room?"

"If I thought that was a viable option, I most certainly would." Eddie took the will from Westley's hands. "But if there is nothing in this document that gives you the right to remain living in my house, I shall banish you from it."

"I don't believe there is any need for rudeness, old chap." Tommy said mildly, moving to the door. He opened it, and finding Malton standing outside, as expected said to the butler. "Could you please send word to the kitchen for a tea tray to be brought to us?"

"I don't want bloody tea!" Eddie returned to his seat and started flicking through the pages of the will. Instead of calming him, Tommy's words seemed to have the very opposite effect. He was now purple with fury.

"If you are going to use such language—" Tommy's voice was no longer calm and reasonable but firm and threaded through with a steely edge. "Perhaps you and Westley should move to another room to discuss the finer points of the will and leave the ladies to their tea."

"You cannot tell me what to do in my own home!" Eddie flung the document onto the side table and thrust himself out of the chair and across the room towards Tommy.

"When you are disrespectful in front of ladies, I can and most certainly will."

"Out!" Eddie pushed open the library door with a loud crash. "Get out!"

"We can take our tea in the drawing room," Evelyn said placatingly. She got to her feet and motioned to everyone. "Let's go through."

Tommy positioned himself between Eddie, and the door as people began to move.

"You first!" Eddie howled, shoving Tommy hard in his back.

Tommy's balance was still slightly affected by the lingering effects of the injury he suffered in the war and he went careening into the doorjamb from the force of Eddie's push, causing Isobel to scream in fright. Turning, Tommy slowly and deliberately approached his cousin. The other man flinched as Tommy reached out and grasped the front of Eddie's shirt.

For a moment, Evelyn wondered if she should intervene, but she need not have worried. Tommy propelled Eddie backwards until he had no choice but to sit back in the wingback chair he had occupied moments earlier.

"Stay there so everyone may safely leave." Tommy removed his hands and brushed them together, as though attempting to removing dirt.

Evelyn hovered near the door after everyone else had left. She watched with a curious mixture of both admiration and concern as Tommy turned back to Eddie. "If you ever lay your hands on me again, you will live to regret it."

Chapter Four

Evelyn clutched Tommy's hand, partly because waiting for the police was straining her nerves, but mostly because she wanted to be sure exactly where he was. Whilst she understood why he had threatened Eddie, the tension that had resulted was unbearable.

Conversation had been stilted whilst they waited for tea to be brought in, no one wanting to draw attention to either Eddie or Lillian's odd behaviour. Whilst Aunt Em, for once, had remained quiet, she had squeezed Tommy's arm to show her appreciation for his gallantry.

In Lillian's absence, Evelyn had poured tea and attempted to create some sense of normality by chatting about the beautiful summer weather and the incredible quality of the gardens. Having received few responses of over one or two words, Evelyn had sat back on the sofa next to Tommy as the increasingly deafening silence invaded every corner of the room.

Opposite, poor Jack Partridge looked particularly out of place. The estate manager balanced a fine china saucer on his lap and held his teacup in the palm of his hand.

"Is all in place for the shoot tomorrow?" she asked him.

What she really wanted to know was where he had gone the evening before, but as they had never had a conversation yet that did not involve shooting or dogs and were not alone, Evelyn didn't really think she would have any luck in getting that question answered.

"Um…yes…Mrs Christie, ma'am."

Eddie's sisters were, of course, all referred to as 'My Lady' as was Aunt Em, and so it seemed that the outside staff who were less used to the proper forms of address, always struggled with what to call her. 'Ma'am' made her feel older than the hills.

She smiled. "Mrs Christie will do just fine."

"Yes, Mrs Christie." Jack smiled back at her, grateful for being putting at his ease. "Everything is ready, should we receive permission for it to go ahead."

Of course, how very silly of her. The weekend would probably not be at all as planned given both Charles's untimely demise and Eddie's incredibly truculent behaviour. Though Eddie liked to shoot, so chances were it would happen unless the police had something to say about the matter.

It was truly the only reason Evelyn had come to Hessleham Hall that weekend. Well, that and her love for her husband. She wouldn't have embarrassed him by not attending, but his family were incredibly difficult people.

She looked around at the other people in the room—the Christie acquaintances weren't much better. The vicar had declined tea and helped himself to the brandy whilst his wife looked as though she were barely holding herself together. Julia Davenport hadn't said a word to anyone, though Evelyn now realised she couldn't remember anyone saying anything to her. Dr Mainwaring was still absent, though Tommy had commented that he expected him back when the police arrived.

"There is much more to life than boring shooting and smelly dogs," Lillian drawled from the doorway.

She looked as though she were auditioning for a part in a Hollywood film. Her blonde hair was styled expertly to wave around her face, her lips painted a bright red, her blouse a size too small, making her breasts much more prominent than decent—especially for daytime. She even seemed to be affecting a more American accent.

Evelyn shrugged. "I prefer dogs to most people."

Lillian raked her gaze over Evelyn, who suddenly felt very plain in her pale blue skirt and cream blouse. "Yes, that makes perfect sense."

Evelyn tamped down her irritation at the other woman's rudeness and decided ignoring her was a much better tactic than engaging in verbal sparring. "Do you shoot, Julia?"

The headmistress's head shot up at the direct question. Her features were too pronounced for her to ever be called pretty. She was what the older generation tended to call 'handsome'. Her eyes were brown and large and were easily her best feature. However, she had a strong nose and lips that were overly full.

"I have had little opportunity, but I'm looking forward to tomorrow." She had a very pleasant voice and an open, friendly manner. Evelyn regretted that she hadn't attempted to talk to her before now. "I hear that your dogs are the best setters in Yorkshire."

"I think you'll find that's the entire country," Tommy chipped in and Evelyn could have kissed him for diffusing the extra tension that Lillian had brought with her remarks.

His comment made everyone laugh, and easy chatter followed.

"Well done, my dears," Emily muttered. "You are quickly becoming my favourite family members."

"Been on the gin again, Aunt Em?" Tommy enquired, then in a fake aside to Evelyn. "That's how she copes with this family."

"Not yet," Em replied with her perfect, very precise diction. She peered at the clock on the mantel. "Though I see it is most definitely nearing time when a tipple would be acceptable."

Malton appeared in the doorway, as usual arriving with the minimum of both noise and fuss. "I have informed the earl who has asked me to let you all know that the police are here. They will take people into the library individually for questioning."

"Now," Em nudged Tommy to his feet, "is most definitely tipple time."

***

The police chose to speak to Tommy first, much to Eddie's disgust.

Although Evelyn was quite sure he had done nothing wrong, and she knew she hadn't, she was horribly nervous. Despite Aunt Em's insistence that the unusual circumstances meant it was acceptable to start pre-dinner drinks in the middle of the afternoon, Evelyn couldn't bring herself to join the older woman. Neither could she bear sitting in the once again silent room.

She excused herself to the kitchen, on the pretext of asking for more tea.

"That girl will never learn how to be a proper lady," Lillian remarked to whoever may listen to her latest catty comment as Evelyn left the room.

If being like Lillian was how one behaved like a proper lady, Evelyn would take that as a compliment.

As Evelyn crept into the busy kitchen, dinner preparation was in full swing. The cook, Mary O'Connell, turned away from the pot she was stirring.

"How can I help you, Mrs Christie?"

The woman's Irish lilt washed over Evelyn and reminded her of the lady from the village who had come into her mother's house when she was a girl. The kindly lady had let Evelyn help her in the kitchen and listened to her childish problems when her mother was too busy with the dogs—which had been most of the time.

"Is there any bread to knead? Vegetables to peel?"

"I can't…"

"I will tell no one," Evelyn pleaded. "I would just very much like something to do."

"Lady Northmoor…"

"Is upstairs in the drawing room. She will never know."

"She's way too la-di-dah to come down here," one of the kitchen maids offered. "She will send for Mrs Chapman if she needs something."

The cook nodded. "I suppose that's right."

"I could make tea?" Evelyn suggested.

Mrs O'Connell pushed a large mixing bowl towards Evelyn. "I was about to make scones. I thought the police would appreciate something light to eat while they do their investigating."

Evelyn nodded and crossed over to the sink. She removed her rings and washed her hands. Returning to the bowl, she mixed the butter into the flour with her fingers. Mrs O'Connell looked over and nodded approvingly.

"You've done that before?"

"Yes, my mother had a lovely lady who came in a few times a week. She let me talk and bake. I find there's nothing like kneading bread to work out a knotty problem in your head."

Mrs O'Connell smiled at Evelyn, but she looked doubtful. No doubt the cook couldn't imagine what a lady such as Evelyn had to worry about. "Well, if you ever have a problem that needs solving, I could always do with an extra pair of hands to knead bread in a morning."

"I shall bear that in mind." Evelyn reached for the sugar and carefully measured out three tablespoons before adding it to the mixture. "Has anyone seen or heard anything unusual over the last few days?"

Her question was asked in an innocent enough voice, but each word was laced with meaning. She kept her head bent over the bowl, concentrating on her task, but she knew the staff would exchange concerned glances.

The same kitchen assistant who'd spoken earlier answered first. "I heard the ladies' maids talking about how the old earl's valet was saying his medicine was missing."

"Now, Nora," the cook admonished. "You can't go saying things like that. It's not our business. The likes of us would do well to keep ourselves to ourselves."

"This is exactly the sort of information I was hoping to hear," Evelyn said smoothly, as she squeezed a lemon and then reached across the table for the vanilla extract. "My husband was in the police before the war and I served from 1915."

"In the police?" Nora's expression was utterly awe struck.

"That's right." Evelyn nodded as she mixed the lemon juice and vanilla extract into a jug of warm milk. "Things are changing for women, mark my words. Until I can do more, I intend to assist my husband to uncover who poisoned the old earl. I'm sure the police will ask him to help with their investigations."

"Well, in that case, I'm sure it's okay to speak about what we know." Nora looked to the cook, rather than Evelyn, for permission.

"Just be aware, miss," Mrs O'Connell addressed Evelyn. "That this is just staff gossip. There may be nothing in it, and you must not believe everything these inexperienced girls tell you."

Evelyn inclined her head. "Indeed. Though I have found that things passed off by men as idle gossip almost always have their basis in truth."

She made a well in the middle of the dry ingredients in the bowl and added the liquid, mixing the wet mixture together with a knife while she waited for the wild hand gestures and muttering behind her to stop.

Evelyn had put flour on the table and tipped the fully mixed dough out of the bowl before Nora spoke again.

"Like I said, the old earl's medicine was missing. I heard tell it was for his heart."

Evelyn looked up at the junior maid. "Might it have been for his blood pressure?"

Nora coloured a little. "I think they said heart but now you mention it, it could have been blood pressure. I don't rightly remember."

"It doesn't matter," Evelyn said soothingly. "I can find that information out from Dr Mainwaring. The important part is knowing that something was missing."

"They kept it on his dressing table and the valet said it was definitely missing when he went up to dress the earl for dinner."

Evelyn rolled out the dough with the rolling pin. "Could you fetch me an egg, please?"

Nora disappeared into the pantry and Mrs O'Connell, as Evelyn had expected, turned back to face her. "You shouldn't listen to things repeated through goodness knows how many lips."

"I take a lot of what I hear with a pinch of salt, Mrs O'Connell, but some of what I'm told definitely needs further investigation." Evelyn waited until she was sure Nora was back in earshot before she continued. "I'm very grateful that you have spoken to me so candidly."

"She's glad you've been honest," Mrs O'Connell muttered towards a confused-looking Nora. "Get Mrs Christie a teacup and a fork."

When Evelyn had the items in front of her, she cracked the egg into the cup and whisked it with the fork and then painted the top of the scones she had already cut from the dough. "It will certainly help the police know where to focus their questions. Thank you, Nora."

When she had finished, Evelyn passed the tray with the scones to Mrs O'Connell to put into the oven. "I'd better go back upstairs before they send out a search party. If we could have some more tea in the drawing room, when you have a minute?"

"Of course, miss." Mrs O'Connell bobbed her head. "I'll do some sandwiches to go with the tea and scones."

"Thank you for letting me invade your kitchen." Evelyn paused at the door. "I shall see you in the morning for the bread kneading."

"And to see what else we have found out?" Nora asked eagerly.

"That would be absolutely champion," Evelyn agreed.

Mrs O'Connell shook her head, but before the cook turned around fully, Evelyn could see an indulgent smile on her face. It didn't hurt to make more friends when one needed eyes and ears in parts of the house where she could not easily go.

Chapter Five

When Evelyn returned to the drawing room, it was to find that things had progressed from a stifling tension to outright hostility. The air crackled with that type of atmosphere that can only be created by words said out loud that should have remained unspoken.

Julia paced over by the long windows that looked out over the garden, Aunt Em nursed a drink that Evelyn very much doubted was the same one that had been in her hand when she left for the kitchen. However, it was Isobel who sat openly weeping that caused her the most concern.

Evelyn looked at Lillian who swirled her amber coloured drink around in the glass, a self-satisfied smirk on her face, that to Evelyn's mind, turned her entire face ugly with the malice that seemed to flow through her today more than ever.

"Afternoon tea will be brought up shortly," she said brightly.

"Oh, do stop being such a martyr, dear," Lillian sneered. "You'll be challenging Saint Isobel over there in a minute."

"What has Isobel done to upset you?" Evelyn asked, moving over to sit next to the vicar's wife, wondering what on earth the nervous woman could have said or done to raise Lillian's ire.

"A conversation about wifely duties that got a little out of hand," Emily said, draining her drink.

"Wifely duties?" Evelyn echoed. It didn't sound as though it was a very seemly conversation for an afternoon in the drawing room.

"I made a simple comment about looking forward to having Christie children in my school," Julia said, still standing over near the windows and not looking as though she wished to come any closer.

"And I said she shouldn't expect that anytime soon," Lillian chipped in. "Then Isobel said it was my duty, especially as Lady Northmoor, to produce an heir. And I simply suggested that while she may be happy being treated as a brood mare, I certainly am not."

"There was a particular comment about the vicar's appearance that I think caused most distress," Emily suggested.

Lillian giggled, a throaty sound that was clearly not a natural sound of mirth. "I called him a fat pig."

Evelyn gasped, and Isobel's distress increased. Even for Lillian, that was a particularly cruel comment.

"Come with me." Evelyn got to her feet and helped Isobel to hers. The vicar's wife sniffed into her handkerchief. "Where are we going?"

"Let's go for a walk," Evelyn suggested.

They left the drawing room together, and Evelyn caught sight of Malton in the hallway. "Could you please ask Doris to bring Nancy downstairs? I wish to take her into the gardens with Mrs Turnbull."

"Nancy is your dog?" Isobel asked and hiccoughed as she choked back a sob and tried to gain control of herself.

"Yes," Evelyn said gently. "My maid, Doris, looks after her while I'm downstairs with the family. I find walks are good for both of us, so I hope you do not mind her joining us while we have a stroll around the garden?"

Doris arrived shortly with an excited Nancy on her lead.

"She's huge," Isobel said doubtfully.

"She's very soft too," Evelyn agreed, stroking the top of Nancy's head. "Let's go outside."

Once in the garden, Evelyn headed to the tree lined area at the very bottom of the lawn. There were times when she took notice of the beautiful flowers and shrubs that were tended to with such care, but not today.

Despite the shady area, Nancy's pink tongue soon lolled out of her mouth, making it look as though she were giving a lop-sided grin. Evelyn wondered how to start a neutral conversation. She thought of, and threw away, several different topics.

"Does she bite?"

Maybe bringing the dog out with someone she already knew to be nervy hadn't been one of her better ideas. "Not at all. She's very friendly."

Evelyn put out a hand and Nancy obligingly gave it a very thorough lick. With the dog facing Evelyn, Isobel reached out trembling fingers and rested them on the dog's back.

"You're right, she is very soft," Isobel commented, becoming braver and running her hand through the black hair on Nancy's back.

"I think her fur is much the same colour as my own hair."

"It is rather." Isobel nodded as she looked at Evelyn's ebony hair. "Although Nancy also has those red patches. They are a quite beautiful hue."

"The Irish setter is actually all red, whilst Gordon setters have mainly black coats with red around their nose, under their chins and at the bottom of their legs and feet." Evelyn loved how the dog's fur shone in the summer sun She was a superb specimen of the breed, but they had not come outside to talk about how fabulous her dog was. "You mustn't take what Lillian says to heart. She likes to believe she is in a play and doesn't stop to think about how her words can hurt people."

"You are very kind," Isobel mumbled. "But I think rather than being an actress, Lillian is just a very bitter and nasty woman."

"Has she been unkind to you before?" Evelyn probed.

"Before when?"

"Sorry," Evelyn rephrased her question. "Before this weekend."

"Not really." Isobel shrugged. "She's never very kind, but this weekend she has been particularly mean."

"Might you have an idea why?"

"No." Isobel shook her head, then looked at Evelyn. "Though she seemed very put out that the earl didn't leave her anything in his will."

"I thought so too," Evelyn mused. "Though why Charles would leave something particularly to his daughter-in-law when he was leaving his entire estate to his son seems very odd, and they were not at all close."

"Is it true that you were in the police during the war?" Isobel asked. "I am certain I remember Oliver telling me that."

"I was," Evelyn confirmed. "Though it wasn't nearly as exciting as I might have hoped. Certainly, Tommy would tell me about the interesting cases he was working on before he went to war, and I wanted to try to do as good a job as he did."

"But you were not allowed?"

Evelyn shook her head. "The few women who could actually join up were not given the same roles as the men. We were really there to provide tea and sympathy to other women, and we didn't get to do anything as involved as investigating."

"I worked during the war, too," Isobel offered.

"What did you do?"

"I worked in the hospital. Not directly with patients, as I was never brave enough to do something like that."

"Oh, I agree." Evelyn nodded enthusiastically. "I think the doctors and nurses were so very brave."

"That's where I met Oliver." Isobel had a faraway look in her eye and a slight smile on her lips, as though remembering something very pleasant but incredibly secret.

"At the hospital?"

Isobel shook her head and the happy memory she seemed to recall vanished from her face entirely. "No."

Evelyn tried desperately to think of something else to say to get the conversation flowing again, but Isobel seemed to have completely shut down. Her fingers absently smoothed the fur on Nancy's head, and she gazed back up towards the house.

"You know, Oliver wasn't always the way he is now."

"I suppose everyone changes over time," Evelyn said weakly.

"We were quite happy until the children started coming so very regularly," Isobel looked on the verge of tears.

"How many do you have?"

"Five." Isobel bit her lip. "In the seven years we have been married and I rather fear that number six may be on its way."

"Gosh, it must exhaust you," Evelyn said before she could stop herself. Once the words were out, she realised they didn't sound very sympathetic or polite.

"It does," Isobel agreed. "But Oliver has absolutely no time for them at all, and less and less for me. He…"

Isobel stopped what she was about to say as the rotund figure of her husband came out of the house and headed towards them.

Privately Evelyn thought Isobel's words were not quite accurate. The vicar must still spend a decent amount of time with his wife because six babies most definitely did not make themselves.

***

After Evelyn and Tommy had both spoken to the police, they met in their room to get ready for dinner. They were hoping to get time with Dr Mainwaring, who had also been asked by the police to stay at the house. Although he had left the house with the body the previous evening, he was a witness to Charles' death and also a suspect, as was everyone else who had been present.

"You didn't know either of the detectives?"

"Apparently, they have been sent from York, which is why they took longer to get here than we expected. It appears those in power want to be sure no one accuses them of bias."

Evelyn gave a most unladylike snort. "That's only because of the murder of that old earl's wife at Scarborough last year. Everyone knew he'd given his wife a shove off the cliff so he would be free to marry his nurse not three months later."

"It was rather a scandal," Tommy agreed. "And it did not give the public a very favourable picture of the police."

"It made them look jolly corrupt."

"Eddie has asked to talk to me," Tommy turned the subject away from his wife's annoyance with the police force. Of course, that went back to them not fully appreciating her efforts or properly utilising her skills during the war.

"Really? What about?"

Tommy moved over to the adjoining door, which he had left slightly open, and quietly closed it.

"Is Brown in there?" Evelyn referred to Arthur Brown, the second footman who also worked as Tommy's valet during their stays at Hessleham Hall.

"Yes, he's patiently waiting to help me dress. Where's Doris?"

"Downstairs feeding Nancy." Evelyn grimaced. "We really are awful as they are trying to do their jobs and we are happily dressing ourselves. Though

Doris doesn't do any of this at home, she's exceptionally good with my hair."

"Eddie wishes to speak to me about officially retiring from the force and running the estate for him."

"Is that not why he employs Partridge?"

"Partridge carries out the day-to-day tasks, but I believe Eddie would like me to plan to make the estate more efficient."

"Was Charles not efficiently running things?"

Tommy nodded. "You know what Eddie is like. If he thinks he can cut corners to make more money for him to spend, then he will. Clearly he wants me to find out how to do that."

"What, then, would Eddie do?"

"Ah, yes," Tommy said. "That would be the question, wouldn't it?"

"And is that what you want to do? Never return to the police and to run this estate? It would be a vast undertaking." Evelyn's voice quivered because she had worked out already what Tommy had not yet said out loud.

Whilst they lived only a mile or so away in the village, running the estate was a full-time job that would never be weekdays only. It would be next to impossible to do it without living at Hessleham Hall.

"We've never really spoken about what I would do once my leg is properly healed," Tommy said, absentmindedly rubbing the aforementioned leg.

"And is it now, darling?" Evelyn asked, moving over and putting a hand over his.

"It is sometimes stiff in a morning, but I don't think it will get any better than it is now. This is the time to decide, particularly with Uncle Charles gone."

"But do you want to do it?" she repeated.

"I think I would be rather good at it."

That wasn't at all the same thing, but it was an answer. "Then it sounds rather like you have decided."

Tommy held Evelyn's face in both of his hands and kissed her lightly on the mouth. "You know I would never make an irrevocable decision about anything without talking to you first."

Because she knew him so very well, and his inner core of decency, Evelyn knew what he would say next.

"It is my duty."

"Then you must do it." Evelyn's heart thundered as she spoke the supportive words, even as she dreaded what would come next.

"I think we would have to give up the cottage,"

She nodded. "I agree. We would have to, if you wanted to give your best efforts to the job. And I know you would do nothing less."

"If you concur, I intend to speak to Eddie and give my agreement but with one condition."

"And what would be?"

"I will tell him I will run the estate, but only if you are given as much space in the stables as you might need for Nancy and however many other dogs you may want."

When they married, Evelyn had reluctantly agreed that one large dog was enough in their small but comfortable cottage and Evelyn's dreams of following in her mother's footsteps and starting her own breeding programme was not possible.

"You would do that for me?"

Tommy looked surprised. "Darling, if I could fly into the sky and return with the moon, should you wish to have it in your hands, I would do it."

"You really are the most romantic man. However did I get so lucky?"

"If I remember correctly, you did not think that when we first met."

"That's because when we first met you were seriously considering arresting me."

"You were climbing into a house through a window." Tommy held out his hands. "It wasn't exactly acceptable behaviour for a lady, nor very innocent looking."

Evelyn laughed at the memory. "Mother had fallen asleep outside with one of the dogs who was having puppies and had locked the house thinking Millicent and I were inside asleep."

"But you had both gone to the picture house and returned home, unable to get in." Tommy finished. He held her gaze for a moment as they both smiled at the shared memory. His face then turned serious once more. "You realise, of course, that the space in the stable and the work I would need to do means we would have to live here. Permanently."

Evelyn shuddered. "Living with Lillian will be hideous."

"It's an enormous house, I'm certain you can spend all day successfully avoiding her."

"You do realise giving me the chance to have my own kennels may mean I take to sleeping outside too, just like my mother?"

"I draw the line at that," Tommy said, a mock stern expression on his face. "There will be no sleeping with dogs in a stable."

"But what if I have a dam who is struggling, or I need to…?"

Tommy reached out and laid a finger on her lips. "Then I shall carry the dog inside, and we will look after her together."

"Have I ever told you what an absolutely glorious man you are?"

"Many times." Tommy preened. "But you may tell me again, if you like."

"I think I shall kiss you instead."

"That would also be acceptable," Tommy replied.

Chapter Six

There was no time to speak to anyone by the time Tommy and Evelyn got downstairs, but shortly after dinner finished and the ladies had left for the drawing room, Eddie took Westley off to the library.

Eddie had ordered that Jack Partridge and the police who were staying at the house whilst they completed their questioning, were to eat in the kitchen with the staff, so that left Tommy in the dining room with the vicar and Dr Mainwaring.

"Is there anything at all they allow you to share about how Charles died?" Tommy asked the village doctor outright.

"The police have said nothing to me about the manner of death being kept a secret."

"We are aware it is poison. Do you know what it was and how it could have got into Charles's system?"

"My belief is that it was hemlock, though the postmortem should verify this. And it could have been administered via any food or drink. No one else has fallen ill, so we must assume Charles was deliberately targeted."

"And there was nothing that could be done for him?" Tommy held up a hand at the other man's frown. "I'm not saying you didn't do your best."

"It wouldn't have mattered what I did. Once the poison was in his system, there was nothing I could do to save him. There is no known cure for hemlock poisoning. He suffered tingling, numbness and eventually paralysis in his extremities and this spread throughout his body ending, of course, with his heart."

Tommy thought for a moment before posing his next question. "And there's no chance we all could have had a bit of poison, but not enough to kill us?"

"Very unlikely. No one else had any symptoms at all."

"Is it tasteless?"

"Actually, no. It has a bitter taste. Its natural form is in a plant that looks similar to parsley, so there have been cases where it has accidentally been added to food. Of course, in a house of this size, there simply is no way for a murderer to successfully ensure their target ate the infected food."

"You said its natural form is a plant. Is it possible to do…something…to change it into a different state? One which…"

"Now see here," the vicar interrupted. "This is not the sort of conversation a chap wants to listen to while he's trying to enjoy his after-dinner port."

Tommy could not think of a polite way to suggest that if Oliver didn't like the conversation, he could take himself off elsewhere, so he simply carried on his line of questioning, reasoning that finding out the identity of a murderer was more important than the upsetting the vicar. "What you're saying then, if I understand you correctly, is that it is more likely that the poison was added to a specific drink so the murderer could be more certain of hitting his target? Like the port, for instance?"

Dr Mainwaring raised his napkin to his lips to hide a smile.

Oliver banged his glass down on the table, drops of the deep red liquid spilling onto the white tablecloth. "Well, really."

He got to his feet, swayed and righted himself by grabbing hold of the edge of the table.

"Are you feeling quite alright?" Dr Mainwaring asked, all traces of mirth now gone from his face as Oliver exhibited similar signs to Charles the night before.

"I am not sure that I am," Oliver moaned. "I think I will go and lay down."

His gait as he made his way to the door was incredibly unsteady.

"I shall come and check on you momentarily," the doctor called to Oliver's retreating back.

"I believe our man of God is simply suffering the effects of too much wine with dinner," Tommy said.

"You are aware the port is not contaminated?"

"Of course," Tommy said easily. "Charles became ill before we started eating. It cannot possibly be the port."

"Jolly unkind of you."

Tommy shrugged. "I want to get to the bottom of this. Charles may not have been the most pleasant of fellows, but he was my uncle."

"So, to answer your earlier question," Dr Mainwaring began. "This particular poison can be in the form of oil, or as a salt."

"And either can be added to food or drink?"

"Yes, but as I noted earlier, there is a taste, but who might imagine that something tasting a little off was because it was contaminated with poison?"

"How long until the symptoms are seen in a victim?"

"My research suggests it would be about thirty minutes following ingestion. So, as I have discussed with the police, this could have happened whilst Charles was in his room or in the drawing room prior to being seated for dinner."

"This rather implicates everyone in the house, including the staff, doesn't it?"

"For the murderer to ensure the only person receiving the lethal dose is the intended target, then yes."

Tommy shook his head. "This is all wrong. What possible reason could any of the staff have for killing Charles?"

"That is rather the conclusion the police arrived at. It makes very little sense. Their intention is to speak to the staff tomorrow." Dr Mainwaring stroked his luxurious moustache, contemplating a question of his own. "Are you intending to help the police solve this dastardly act?"

"Alas not." Tommy shook his head. "They have told me that the reason they are here, from York, is to ensure the matter is investigated independently of the local police force. They specifically do not want my help."

"And yet you are determined to assist in any event?"

"As I said earlier, Charles is family." Speaking of his uncle in the past tense still felt incredibly odd, even though Eddie was flexing his 'new earl' authority in every conceivable way. "It wouldn't feel right to me if I didn't do everything in my power to uncover the perpetrator."

"Well, I wish you luck. At this stage, it seems an absolutely impossible mystery."

Tommy nodded. "They all seem that way, at first."

"I should go check on the vicar." Dr Mainwaring got reluctantly to his feet.

"He does not exactly fulfil my notions of what a vicar should be and how they should act."

"Nor mine," the doctor agreed.

Tommy decided the vicar definitely had secrets and it was important that they be uncovered.

***

"Here I am!" Evelyn announced early the next morning from the open door to the kitchen.

"My goodness, Mrs Christie. I didn't really expect that you would come," Mrs O'Connell flustered.

"A promise is a promise," Evelyn said in a sing-song voice. "And it must be kept. Now I hope you have plenty of dough for me to knead, as I'm feeling very energetic this morning."

"And ready to hear a lot of gossip," the cook muttered, not quite quiet enough that Evelyn failed to hear.

"I do like to talk while I work," Evelyn agreed.

"I have dough ready to knead. I was going to do it myself, but if you're insistent, I'll pour us both a nice cup of tea. I will be glad of the help and the company."

"What a delight." Evelyn smiled and crossed over to the sink to wash her hands.

"It does so happen I think Nora has heard something you may like to know," Mrs O'Connell said, pouring a cup of tea for Evelyn and putting it next to the bowl containing the risen dough.

Evelyn took off her rings and placed them carefully out of the way so they would not get covered in either dough or flour. Next, she sprinkled flour on the table and set about kneading the air bubbles from the bread dough. "Where is my newest friend?"

"Nora is getting vegetables from the larder. She's been gone for a while, but she's probably busy mooning again." Mrs O'Connell leaned closer, as though she was about to impart a great secret. "Nora is in love!"

"Oh, how thrilling." Evelyn smiled. "There's nothing quite so special as a girl's first love."

"Ah yes, Mr Christie is a very dashing man."

"Mr Christie is an absolute…" Nora stopped speaking and blushed bright red as she saw Evelyn sitting at the table.

Evelyn waved a flour covered hand in the girl's direction. "You can finish your sentence. My husband is a very decent looking fellow, I know. I'm very lucky."

"Oh Mrs Christie…ma'am…" Nora stumbled. "I didn't mean any disrespect."

"None taken," Evelyn said breezily. "Any woman with two eyes in their head can see what a catch my Tommy is."

"Indeed!" Mrs O'Connell spluttered.

"I know what you are thinking," Evelyn went on. "That it's not proper I should speak to you so openly. Well, I will soon live here permanently and so I mean you to be my friends. Therefore, I can assure you that it is most acceptable."

"But…"

"Yes, I know," Evelyn agreed. "If the new Earl of Northmoor, or his wife, were to find out, they would certainly not agree. However, I have no intention of breaking any confidences or speaking out of turn. Shall we continue?"

"I'm not at all sure where we were, Mrs Christie, ma'am." The cook shook her head.

"Ah, I was about to correct you, I believe." Evelyn really wished they would all feel comfortable enough to call her something other than Mrs Christie or ma'am but she dare not shock them any more than she already had by asking that they call her by her given name. "You suggested Mr Christie was my first love."

"He wasn't?"

"Oh, good golly, no." Evelyn laughed. "My first love was the coal merchant's son."

"Oh, Mrs Christie, really?" Nora giggled.

"Indeed." Evelyn smiled as she pounded the dough and twisted it around, before pummelling it again. "I simply admired him from afar. If he had ever spoken anything to me other than 'mornin', I think I may well have swooned."

"That's exactly how I feel," Nora confessed. "Every time Albert so much as looks in my direction."

"The butcher's boy," Mrs O'Connell explained.

"Do tell me more," Evelyn said.

"Well, I was talking to him about your Nancy," Nora began. "Seeing as how Doris brings her downstairs just after breakfast and how we like to try to keep some extra sausages back for her. Doris says so long as she doesn't get fat, you won't mind."

"Not at all," Evelyn agreed.

"And he said he would bring a whole extra string of sausages up this very day, just for Nancy."

"I don't expect that's the only reason he's making an extra trip up here," the cook suggested. "You make sure Mrs Chapman doesn't catch you and there's no funny business going on."

"Oh, no." Nora coloured again. "If he tried to steal a kiss, I think I would be like Mrs Christie here and I'd swoon right to the ground."

"I think you've about beaten the life out of that." Mrs O'Connell peered over at the dough Evelyn was working on.

"Do you have more?" Evelyn asked. "I believe we are just getting started with the information sharing."

"Oooh." Nora clapped a hand over her mouth. "I was so excited to tell you about Nancy and the sausages that I clean forgot to tell you what I've been completely bursting to tell you."

"Thank you, Mrs O'Connell," Evelyn said as the cook took away the dough she'd finished and passed her a fresh mound. She took a sip of tea. "This sounds intriguing."

"Well, Albert says as how the butcher has got a good supply of rabbit very suddenly. And cheap too."

"Really?" Evelyn encouraged, her mind wondering where the girl was going with this information and how it could possibly have any bearing on Charles's murder.

"Seems they are being sold by Geoffrey Beckett," Nora paused for dramatic effect. "And everyone knows that he poaches on this land. On Hessleham Hall land."

"Goodness, so you believe this Geoffrey is stealing?"

"I certainly do. And furthermore, Albert heard the butcher talking to his wife, saying as how the supply is never-ending because Beckett has some sort of scheme going with Jack Partridge!" Nora finished triumphantly.

"The estate manager knows this Beckett fellow is poaching?"

"Now, Mrs Christie, you can't go saying anything. This is third hand information at best," the cook protested.

"Oh, not at all. It's hardly my business if a few rabbits go missing. Certainly, it is my understanding they repopulate rather quickly." Evelyn concentrated on the new dough in front of her. The estate manager was a completely unknown part of this puzzle. She didn't know him at all, but she would make sure she had as innocent a conversation as possible with him during the shoot that day, should it go ahead.

"I wouldn't want Albert to get into trouble." Nora looked worried, almost as though she wished she had said nothing.

"Of course not," Evelyn assured the girl. "I'm sure you all know that the earl has asked Tommy to help him out with the business. If Jack has something going on, that isn't above board, my Tommy will soon find out. So never fear, nothing we have spoken about this morning will be repeated."

"Do you think it's possible Jack bumped off the old earl because he found out what Geoffrey and Jack were up to?" Mrs O'Connell wondered.

"I think it's entirely possible," Evelyn agreed. "It would certainly be a motive. I am just not sure he would have the means to do such a thing."

"The means?" Nora asked.

"Oh, I mean the ability to get hold of poison and give it only to the earl so no one else got ill. There are some people who could walk around the house without suspicion, but if Jack Partridge went anywhere near any of the upstairs rooms, it would look very odd, wouldn't it?"

Nora nodded. "Someone would be sure to notice."

"The upstairs maids would have said something," the cook added. "Though maybe you should talk to Mrs Chapman to see if she knows anything. She knows most of what goes on in this house."

"I have never yet spoken to that lady," Evelyn said pensively. "How would you suggest I best approach her?"

"Oh, that's easy," Mrs O'Connell said, a mischievous glint in her eye. "Tell her she would be helping you out and Mrs Lillian...that is...Lady Northmoor should know nothing about your conversation."

"Mrs Chapman is not keen on the new Lady Northmoor?"

The staff looked at each other and laughed uproariously. "She has been making herself very unpopular with her demands. I'm surprised there hasn't been something jolly unpleasant put in that cream she slaps all over her face on an evening."

"Oh dear, that bad?"

"You can't imagine. She should watch herself or, mark my words, she'll be next."

Evelyn didn't pass comment on the cook's last words as she could see the minute they were out of the older lady's mouth, she wished she hadn't said them.

Evelyn wished she had the words to assure the cook that there wasn't a single person in the household who didn't feel exactly the same about Lillian. Whilst she herself didn't have any particular feeling about another death in the house, she did feel very uneasy about the swirling depth of emotions and she was just as certain that something else terrible would happen very soon.

Chapter Seven

"How dare they!" Eddie raged, fury emanating from his body as he stamped across the hardwood floor of the library.

"They said we could go ahead tomorrow," Tommy said placatingly.

"There should have been three days of shooting," Eddie carried on complaining. "Now we will be lucky if we manage one."

"There's lots of other days…"

"We always shoot for three days over a weekend when the season opens." Eddie whirled around to face Tommy and thrust out an accusatory finger. "Oh, you wouldn't understand what family tradition means. You are not the Earl of Northmoor."

Tommy was jolly glad he wasn't if it meant having to get so cross about missing a day's shooting because the police were still investigating the death of your father. He took a deep breath before again trying to mollify his cousin.

"Maybe we could talk about what you need me to do to help you run the estate?"

Eddie stared at Tommy for a long moment. "I don't really need you to help me."

"Oh?" Tommy wasn't quite sure what to say to that. Eddie had been very clear the day before that he wanted to discuss arrangements with him. "I thought that was the reason you wanted to speak with me today?"

"You're the spare heir, for now, so I think it is right you should know how the estate runs. And, with your background, I know that I can trust you."

Tommy thought that was possibly the nicest thing Eddie had ever said to him. It was also, more than likely, the nicest thing he would ever say to him from that moment on.

"What exactly do you need from me?"

"I want you to learn all about the estate and get on with the job of sorting it out," Eddie said impatiently.

Tommy was beginning to understand how he and his cousin had been approaching this issue from very different viewpoints. "It sounds rather like you don't want to be involved at all, but you want me to take care of the estate completely?"

"Exactly that!" Eddie answered as though it was completely obvious. "Of course, you run anything important by me, and I make all the decisions."

"And Evelyn and I live here so I am able to carry out my duties on a daily basis?"

"Yes, you must," Eddie snapped. "I don't want to send to the village every time I need you."

Tommy closed his eyes in defeat. With every single word Eddie spoke, his own freedoms were disintegrating. He would be at his cousin's beck and call every minute of every day. Yet what else could he do?

The situation was precarious. Should Eddie fail to have an heir of his own, it would fall upon Tommy's own son to run an estate of which he, Tommy, would have no working knowledge. If Eddie had a son, he would need someone to help him learn how to be the master of his estate, and it did not appear Eddie had any desire to perform that particular function.

If he refused, he could go back to his work in the police force, which he had enjoyed immensely, but it would mean he was turning his back on his own family. However, working with Eddie could mean another repeat of his behaviour after the will was read—Tommy did not want to put either himself, or Evelyn, in such a precarious situation.

"Then I have conditions," Tommy said firmly.

Eddie's brows drew together, and he finally sat in the chair opposite Tommy, seemingly exhausted from his ranting. "What might they be?"

His cousin's voice was cautious, but Tommy didn't think he would have a problem with any of the things he was about to insist upon. He held up one hand. "Number one, and this is the most important of my points: there must be no physical violence. That means no shoving, as you did yesterday. Not towards me, or anyone else. If that happens, we leave. Immediately."

Eddie looked suitably chastened, Tommy thought, for maybe one of the first times in his life. Certainly, he had never seen Eddie look ashamed before. Maybe all the other man needed was to be reminded how a gentleman should behave every now and again.

"Fair enough."

That wasn't an apology, and Tommy was aware there wouldn't be one for Aunt Em either, but he thought this was maybe the best they could hope for right now. "Point two," Tommy held up another finger. "I want space allocated in the stables for Evelyn, so she can begin a breeding programme. This will also help you when you have shoots as there will be dogs trained by family, who can be trusted and who will have been reared correctly."

There had been instances of dogs running all over and ruining shoots because they had not been trained by someone who understood the correct processes and variants of hunt, set and retrieve.

"I've already said she can have space," Eddie was back to being belligerent, a frustrated look now on his face.

"In return, I will deal with any issues. Perhaps we should have a weekly meeting so I can keep you up to date?"

"That would seem more than adequate." Eddie agreed, backtracking immediately on his earlier stipulation that Tommy run absolutely every decision past him. "Are you finished?"

"Not quite," Tommy said placidly, knowing his cousin was running out of patience and really wanting to get his final condition agreed. The first two were the most important, of course, but he wanted the last one for himself.

"Well hurry up, I need to speak to the police again."

"My last request is that I want to have my own space to work in. I do not wish to have a little corner of the library where I may be disturbed every time someone wants to clean and dust or wants to look for a book."

Not that many people in the house used the library to actually acquire books, let alone sit in it and read. The only person he could think of that did that was Evelyn. But still, he wanted a space to work in, to call his own.

"Where did you have in mind?" Eddie spoke as though the house didn't have lots of rooms that were either no longer used, or very under-used.

"I thought the old smoking room. We don't really use it anymore, and it's near the side entrance so I wouldn't have to come in through the main entrance if I'm dirty."

"Yes," Eddie said grandly. "I don't want you coming in through the servants' entrance either. You're a gentleman. We don't want people getting confused as to your place."

"No," Tommy agreed. "We wouldn't want anyone to forget their place."

Eddie stared at Tommy again, as though he was certain there was an undercurrent in his words, but he wasn't sure what they were. Finally, he seemed to give up trying to work out any other meaning. "Right."

"I thought we could set that room up immediately and the police can use it whilst they are here, which frees up the library, and I will take over when they have left."

"We?"

"I meant 'we' as in the family. I am more than happy to take care of all the arrangements. In fact, if you would like, I would be quite prepared to liaise with the police regarding their investigations on behalf of the family, to save you the trouble?"

"They are rather tiresome." Eddie nodded his agreement. "Perhaps, as you speak their language, you can get them to agree to us shooting today?"

"Why don't I see what I can do?" Tommy suggested smoothly.

"Is that all?" Eddie enquired.

"Almost." Tommy arranged his face into an earnest expression. "I wondered if you would have any idea whatsoever as to how your father could have ingested the poison that killed him?"

"What are you implying?" As usual, Eddie jumped to entirely the wrong conclusion, which was mostly why Tommy hadn't tried to get any information out of him sooner.

"Absolutely nothing, old man," Tommy assured him. "Simply that you know your father and his habits best. I thought you might have seen or heard something out of the ordinary. Anything at all? The sooner we crack this mystery, the sooner we can get the police out of Hessleham Hall and get on with our lives."

"And the season's shooting," Eddie grumbled.

"Does that mean you know nothing that may help?"

"Nothing." Eddie confirmed in a voice so unlike his usual brusque tone that Tommy was sure his cousin knew something that could be useful—now all he had to do was work out a way to get the information out of him.

***

"Have you heard that Tommy and I will be residing at the house permanently?" Evelyn asked Lillian in a bright voice to mask how very reluctant she was to speak with her sister-in-law.

Tommy had told her he had learned nothing new from Eddie, so Evelyn was even more determined to get some useful information out of Lillian.

"How incredibly tiresome," Lillian drawled.

Evelyn hadn't expected excitement from the other woman or proclamations of feminine solidarity suggesting make-up and hair styling evenings, borrowing each other's clothes and becoming close friends but the downright hostility was upsetting even as Evelyn reminded herself that she really didn't care for Lillian one little bit.

"I'm sorry you feel that way." Evelyn folded her hands in her lap, wishing she wasn't one of those people who wanted everyone to like her and then allowed it to bother her if they did not.

"I suppose if you will be here all the time, we will all have to get used to the smell of wet dog and become accustomed to picking dog hair from our clothes all the time?"

Evelyn was absolutely certain that Lillian's lady's maid would brush any stray hairs there happened to be from her clothing, and Evelyn would never allow a situation to arise wherein Lillian could be bothered by Nancy.

She decided to leave that topic where it was and move onto the questions she wanted to ask. "You seemed very upset yesterday when you discovered Charles had not left you anything in his will."

"I had been assured he would," Lillian said lazily, trailing a hand over her perfectly styled hair. "It was certainly a great disappointment."

"Did Eddie tell you that you were to inherit something?"

"He did." Lillian had an amused smile on her face. "But he was about as useless at securing that as he is at everything he does."

"Oh dear," Evelyn said, not knowing what the correct response to Lillian's sarcasm should be.

"Though he's not completely hopeless." Lillian gave a tinkering laugh. "He's got your husband doing his job for him, so that will certainly give him more time to chase the girls in the village."

"Oh, Lillian." Evelyn couldn't help her gasp of shock. "I'm sure that isn't true."

"And I'm equally sure that it is. He has always been the most frightful philanderer."

"But I don't understand." Evelyn was aware how terribly naïve she sounded, but she couldn't help herself. She just didn't comprehend why people would marry and then carry on with other people. And, despite her acid tongue, Lillian was quite beautiful. Why would Eddie want anyone else but her?

"Evelyn," Lillian drew out the name, as though talking to a child. "Don't you wonder why, after all of these years of marriage, there are no heirs in waiting? Eddie has his fun, and I have mine. We just don't have it together."

Evelyn couldn't help herself. "How awful. How absolutely dreadful."

"You are such a child! Have you never wanted…?" Lillian paused. "Oh, of course you haven't, Eddie is…well…Eddie, but you got Tommy. Quite the jewel in the Christie crown. I often wish I'd seen him before Eddie."

For one awful moment, whilst the fury of burning hot jealousy ran through her veins, Evelyn wanted to pull Lillian's hair from its perfectly arranged style. She didn't want her horrible, immoral sister-in-law anywhere near her husband. Why on earth had she agreed to live in the same house as this poisonous human being?

"Hmm." Lillian smiled in a cat-that-has-got-the-cream way. "Maybe there is more to you than meets the eye. You looked positively *murderous* just then."

"Can't you just stop it, just for a moment?" Evelyn asked, frustration getting the best of her.

"Oh, go on." Lillian motioned with a hand. "You want to ask me questions and be an amateur detective. That's why you're here talking to me so get on with it. Ask me your questions."

She was much brighter than Evelyn had given her credit for. The overdone make-up, perfect hair and acid tongue hid a sharp mind.

"Do you know how Charles could have been poisoned?" Evelyn asked.

"One would imagine it must have been put into his pre-dinner brandy. He had one every evening. It wouldn't take too much effort for someone to pour in the poison."

"And then afterwards? It would poison anyone else who had it."

Lillian shrugged. "I suppose. Now, if you want to know where the Earl of Northmoor and myself were before dinner, I was getting ready, but I don't know where Eddie was. Though, of course, the poison could have been added at any time during the day before Charles took his habitual drink before dinner."

Frustration wrapped itself around Evelyn. Tommy had reported feeling exactly the same way after he had spoken to Eddie. The mystery just didn't seem to make any sense at all. Maybe that was because they couldn't rule anyone out. Almost anyone could've slipped into the drawing room and added poison to the brandy, as Lillian suggested.

"Is that it?" Lillian asked. "You don't have any other probing questions for me?"

Evelyn shook her head, but as she was about to leave the room, she could think of only one thing she wanted to ask. Lillian had already made her contempt for Evelyn clear, so Evelyn didn't think she could damage their relationship any more with the brutally honest question that hovered on her lips.

She shrugged, deciding it definitely couldn't make anything worse, and she wanted to know the answer. "Are you having an affair with Westley Harrison?"

Lillian's head snapped up, and she stared directly at Evelyn before smiling slyly and making her way over to the drinks tray in the corner of the room. "Let's hope no one has been adding anything unpleasant to the gin!"

She poured herself a drink that was much more gin than tonic and held up the bottle to offer Evelyn a drink.

"No, thank you."

"Of course not." Lillian laughed. The blatantly sarcastic sound was beginning to get on Evelyn's nerves. "It's much too early in the day for you, isn't it, darling?"

Evelyn could have told her she just didn't much fancy sharing a drink and prolonging their time together, but she didn't feel the need to hurt someone else's feelings just because she could. Though, in retrospection, she very much doubted Lillian had any feelings that could be hurt.

"Are you going to answer my question?"

"Of course." Lillian sipped her drink, nodded in approval, then drank the rest in one long, greedy gulp. "I can confirm that I am not having an affair with Westley, though that's not because he doesn't want to. I am, however, enjoying a passionate string of liaisons with Jack Partridge."

Evelyn opened her mouth to dispute the truth of Lillian's words. Aunt Em was sure Westley was the man in Lillian's life and she herself had seen them together, though, of course, that didn't have to mean

anything. They could genuinely have been talking. Yet Evelyn wasn't sure that she believed that.
How on earth did one tell someone who had just admitted to an affair you thought they were a liar?

Chapter Eight

Evelyn sat with Aunt Em on one of the many benches dotted throughout the garden, breathing in the scent of the flowers and trying to relax after her discussions with Lillian.

"Lillian was difficult?" Aunt Em asked.

"She was…" Evelyn paused, trying to find the right words. "Her usual self."

Em nodded. "I'm sure. Do you think she told you the truth?"

"I think the same as Tommy did after he spoke with Eddie. Some truth was told, but there are also things that they are both still hiding."

"Though, of course, their secrets do not necessarily have to be anything to do with the murder," Em said wisely. "It could just be that there are things they do not wish to share."

"Interestingly enough—" Evelyn shuffled on the hard wood of the bench to get more comfortable. "Lillian told me she absolutely is not having an affair with Westley, but with Jack!"

Evelyn made no attempt to keep the outrage from her voice. Lillian had been so casual and matter of fact with her confession.

"Oh dear," Em mused. "I had thought that particular dalliance was over."

"You knew about Lillian and Jack?"

"Of course."

"Aunt Em, how?"

"You think because I am an old lady I don't see and hear what is going on around me? You don't imagine that there may be occasions when I am sitting in a chair in the library, facing away from the door, and hear people coming in and talking about things they would wish I had not been privy to?"

"You will tell me next that you are also aware there are whispers that Eddie isn't a faithful husband too."

Aunt Em laughed at this. "My dear child, I would think the entire village knows that."

"Goodness," Evelyn said. "Am I so terribly naïve?"

"I would think that perhaps you have not yet learned the art of incredible attention to detail."

"Is that the same as what is commonly known as being a nosey parker?"

"Evelyn!" Aunt Em said sharply. "When one is a lady, one is never nosey. However, there is nothing at all wrong with being very observant. In fact, in this house, observance may well lead to a longer life."

Evelyn sighed. "It is all rather worrying, isn't it?"

"I hardly dare put food or drink in my mouth," Em agreed.

"Though we have done nothing to cause someone to want to murder us, surely?"

"There are lots of reasons for murder, and not all of them logical." Em put a hand on Evelyn's. "A person may be killed because of what they know, so it may have nothing to do with whether they are a likeable person. You must be very careful with the questions you are asking. If you learn too much about the wrong person, your life could be in danger."

Evelyn hadn't thought about things that way. She had simply thought finding out who the murderer was would prove, if only to herself, that she would have made a very good policewoman and should've been kept on after the war.

"There's no danger of that," Evelyn assured the other woman. "Tommy and I haven't been able to find out anything, really. At least, nothing that makes sense or seems very relevant."

"Sometimes information doesn't appear pertinent at all, right until the moment when it is. In fact, by that time, it can be positively crucial."

"I don't think I understand." Evelyn frowned.

"People are mostly creatures of habit and routine. A murder such as Charles' could only have been pulled off successfully because of those two things. It's likely he was poisoned because someone knew his habit of having a brandy before dinner every evening. Now, it therefore follows that something will be missing, or out of place, or perhaps even present that shouldn't be. And it may seem very insignificant."

Evelyn thought about what Aunt Em had said. It made perfect sense, except she wasn't sure of what she should be seeing. Or not seeing. Her head hurt with all the fresh information she had been told. Perhaps the best thing she could do at this point would be to look at Charles's bedroom. After all, the police had already done the same thing, and the room was not out of bounds, so there was no reason she shouldn't.

"So, do you think Charles was killed because of something he knew?"

"I don't think Charles had very many secrets." Em shook her head. "Though he wasn't a very nice man, so he could have been killed simply because someone didn't like him."

"You didn't gain at all from Charles dying. You already had the items Charles left to you in his will?"

Aunt Em pulled a face. "The items he specifically mentioned were not his to leave to me. They were my mother's and therefore never even belonged to the Christie family. My nephew, unfortunately, believed that because he was the Earl of Northmoor, he was not only in charge of the house and the land but also the people and their private possessions."

"Do you think Eddie will really try to turn you out of the house?"

Aunt Em raised one elegant shoulder. "That boy is too much like his father and not at all like his poor mother. Nothing he does will surprise me."

"What was his mother like?"

"Florence was a beautiful, gentle creature. The absolute opposite of Lillian. Despite having nearly as many children as Queen Victoria, she ran this house like it was a military manoeuvre. Everyone adored her."

"It sounds as though you were friends?"

"Yes," Em nodded. "We were. As you know, I never married, so Florence was the closest thing I ever had to a daughter. We were very close."

"She died very young." Evelyn stated it as a fact, not a question.

"She gave birth to seven children in thirteen years, with other pregnancies in-between. Charles wanted a son. And what Charles wanted, Charles got." Aunt Em closed her eyes. "However, she adored her children. I still don't believe after all of these years that she took too much of her sleeping draught on purpose."

"Oh," Evelyn murmured and put a hand over her mouth. "How dreadful. I didn't realise…"

"You wouldn't have any reason to know." Em's grip on Evelyn's hands became stronger as her sad memories took hold. "Eddie was just a baby then, Tommy not even born, and it wasn't something Charles ever talked about."

"And Charles?" Evelyn hardly dared to put the words into a sentence, but she forced herself to try. "Could Charles have given Florence too much of her night-time powders?"

Em's eyes glittered with anger. "I don't suppose we shall ever know."

Evelyn blinked tears from her eyes. She had always wondered what had happened to Charles' wife, but had never thought the truth would be so tragic. Neither had she known the depth of Em's feelings for the other woman.

She was becoming very fond of Aunt Em, but what she had now learned did not mean that she could strike Em from her list of suspects. Charles's aunt certainly had the three essential reasons to stay a suspect.

Means.

Motive.

Opportunity.

***

Tommy caught up with Oliver in the billiard room. Evelyn had briefed him about the conversation she had with Isobel and so had some questions following on from that, as well as several of his own.

"How are you holding up?" Tommy asked to open up the conversation. "With the police in the house and all?"

"I'm all right but I think Isobel is eager to get home to the children."

"Do you have a nanny at home?"

"Of course," Oliver answered with a sneer, as though it was a particularly stupid question.

Not for the first time, Tommy wondered why Charles had invited Oliver and Isobel for the weekend. They were not at all the kind of people his uncle had usually been friendly with. Though perhaps friendly was too intimate a word for the people who frequented Hessleham Hall. Charles had an extensive list of people who corresponded with him, particularly during shooting season, but Tommy didn't think many of them would claim the descriptor 'friend'.

Neither did it appear that there was anything a country vicar could do for Charles, which took away another possible reason for his presence.

"Isobel was talking to my wife about how you met at the hospital before the war," Tommy said nonchalantly.

Of course, Isobel had told Evelyn nothing of the sort. In fact, she had specifically not said how they had met and been secretive about the subject.

Oliver got to his feet and moved over to pour himself a particularly large double brandy. "Well, that is unfortunate."

"Is it?" Tommy did his best not to sound as confused as he felt.

"Rather." Oliver drank the amber liquid in one go before pouring himself more.

Tommy wondered if the vicar ate and drank as much in his own home as he did at Hessleham Hall. If so, it was a wonder the Turnbulls could feed and clothe one child, let alone five. Though, Tommy suddenly realised, Oliver had said they had a nanny. He wasn't particularly up on the subject, but it certainly seemed to him that Oliver would struggle to afford a nanny on a vicar's salary. This was a subject that he would definitely need to explore further.

"Well, it was all so very long ago now," Tommy suggested, not wanting Oliver to guess he had absolutely no idea where this conversation was going and hoping the other man would start talking.

"As you well know from developments this weekend, it doesn't matter how many years have gone by when murder, or suspected murder, is involved."

"Yes." Tommy nodded, even more bewildered. "I can see that."

Oliver came to sit in one of the leather chairs near the fireplace. He held the decanter of brandy in one hand and the tumbler he was drinking from in the other. "Everything was very different back then."

"The war certainly changed everything," Tommy murmured, not wanting to stop Oliver from talking but feeling a need to say something.

Oliver took another sip of his drink. "Isobel was bright and vibrant. Funny and outgoing."

It was as though Oliver were describing someone Tommy did not know. None of those words sounded a bit like Isobel. In fact, they were the total opposite of the vicar's wife. Tommy was desperate to ask what had gone wrong, but there wasn't a delicate way to ask how Isobel had turned into such a dowdy, plain and downright neurotic woman.

As it happened, Tommy didn't need to say any more as the brandy was loosening Oliver's tongue very well without Tommy's interference. "Of course, she's having an affair."

Tommy blinked. Isobel—affair? What a ludicrous idea. Though from what Evelyn had told him, it seemed that there wasn't anyone in the house, or village, who wasn't having some sort of extramarital dalliance.

"I'm sure you're mistaken."

"She thinks I don't know," Oliver said, as though Tommy hadn't spoken. "But how can a chap not know when his wife is off with another man?"

Tommy had no idea, but the very thought of another man touching Evelyn made him quite furious. "Surely—"

"I know my own wife!" Oliver cut in, anger now in his voice. "One day a week, Isobel goes out to the shops but on that day, she dresses up and wears perfume. Only we have everything delivered. She has no need to go to the shops."

"Perhaps she just wants an afternoon out by herself?" Tommy suggested.

"In her best frock?" Oliver scoffed. "I have watched her leave the house. She walks down the lane looking excited and happy."

Oliver crashed his tumbler onto the side table next to him. "It is exactly how she used to look when we first met."

To Tommy's horror, Oliver put his head in his hands and wept. Awkwardly, he reached over and patted the other man's back. "Now, see here, I'm sure there has been a terrible misunderstanding."

Oliver shook his head morosely. "You don't understand. She thinks I don't know. But, of course, I do. It's happened so many times before."

"She's had lots of other affairs?" Tommy really couldn't help the shock in his voice.

"Not that," Oliver managed between sobs of complete desolation. "She is to have a child. And I can tell you quite categorically that it is not mine."

Tommy closed his eyes. In his time in the police, he had seen and heard some things that had left him speechless, but this was right up there with the worst of his experiences. Oliver had literally fallen apart in front of his eyes, and Tommy had no idea whatsoever what he could say or do to ease the other man's distress.

Chapter Nine

Evelyn was stunned by the information she and Tommy had learned that day. It appeared that no one staying at Hessleham Hall that weekend was quite as they seemed. Even Aunt Em had been harbouring deep secrets.

Tommy was taken aback by Oliver's admissions. It seemed very unlikely they had met at the hospital during the war, that would not have given them enough time to have five children though, as Evelyn pointed out, twin pregnancies may have made it possible.

The revelation that Isobel was having an affair had really shocked Evelyn. The other woman did not seem at all the type. Though Evelyn had already realised that she herself quite clearly did not have any idea what type of woman indulged in extra-marital relationships.

Was it at all possible that Isobel had been seeing Charles, or even Eddie? If that were the case, it would go some way to explaining how very nervous Isobel seemed. Of course, Charles was quite a bit older than Isobel and it had been suggested that Eddie liked to pursue innocent village girls. The vicar's wife definitely did not fall into that category. It would be an excellent idea to visit the kitchen again. They certainly seemed to know what was going on in the house.

Tommy had not found out why Oliver and Isobel had been invited that weekend, so Evelyn was doubly determined to find out why Julia Davenport was spending the weekend with them.

After some enquiries, Evelyn was told by Malton that Miss Davenport liked to take a book to read down at the bottom of the garden next to the small stream that ran along the southern edge of the estate.

Evelyn found Julia sitting on a blanket with a book on her lap, but instead of reading she was staring off across the stream at something Evelyn could not see. As she approached, Julia turned to face her, a frown on her face.

"I'm sorry if I'm disturbing you," Evelyn said, peering off into the distance to see what had caught Julia's attention.

"Not at all," the schoolteacher said. She patted the blanket. "Do sit down."

Evelyn sat and decided jumping straight in was a lot easier than trying to carefully pick her words and dance around the questions she really wanted to ask. "What were you looking at so intently over the stream?"

"Two people were kissing very passionately," Julia said in her no-nonsense, clipped tones. Evelyn could imagine her being a very good schoolteacher.

"Shocking," Evelyn murmured. "Were you able to see who it was?"

Julia raised a hand to shield her eyes from the sun. "No, they were over there under that tree. I do believe one of those involved was our new Lady Northmoor. The female definitely had fair hair."

Evelyn tried to think who else it could have been. Isobel had mousy hair and whilst the kitchen assistant, Nora, had fair hair, she didn't think the young girl would indulge in passionate embraces under a tree. For a start, Mrs O'Connell would surely have a tight control on her time and Nora's own reaction when talking about Albert suggested that even a peck on the cheek would be something the girl would think too forward. Of course, the kitchen maid's clothing would also mean it very unlikely Julia would mistake Nora for Lillian.

"Goodness, I have never seen Eddie and Lillian be so very open about their affection for each other." Evelyn hoped her voice sounded as innocent as she meant it to be.

"Oh, the gentleman wasn't the earl." Julia shook her head for emphasis. "Whoever it was had dark hair. Eddie's is quite red, particularly in the sun."

Eddie would insist his hair was strawberry blond to anyone who dared to suggest he was a redhead. Either way, there was no way he would be mistaken for a dark-haired man, even at a distance.

"Oh," Evelyn said, wishing she could think of something more intelligent to say.

"I rather imagine it was Westley Harrison," Julia said matter of factly.

"I had heard that they were enjoying a lot of each other's company lately."

Julia snorted. "I don't think there's a lady for miles who hasn't enjoyed that gentleman's company at one time or another."

"That sounds a little like you may have had an unfortunate experience with him yourself."

"You could say that," Julia looked wistful for a moment. "Of course, he's very good looking and incredibly dashing."

"That is true," Evelyn agreed. "Though I must say he's not quite as handsome as he believes he is."

"You don't think so?"

"No," Evelyn said. "I think that when one has an unkind heart, it diminishes their physical beauty. In the same way as Lillian is a very beautiful woman, she can also be very unpleasant in her dealings with other people and it negatively affects her beauty, in my opinion. Were you perhaps out here waiting to meet Westley yourself?"

Julia looked at Evelyn for so long, Evelyn didn't think she would answer. "I hoped he may wish to see me again, but he does not appear to notice me in that way anymore."

Evelyn felt very sorry for Julia. It had been a long time since the coal merchant's son broke her heart and she had been just a girl. No doubt having one's heart broken when you were truly in love and as an adult was very much worse. And she believed from Julia's demeanour that she had most definitely been in love with Westley.

"Has it been very difficult being here this weekend with Westley when you so clearly wish to be back in his affections?"

"Yes," Julia breathed, tears shimmering in her eyes. "It has been positively torturous!"

"Could you have excused yourself and not come?"

Julia coloured a little at this suggestion, which Evelyn immediately felt was very odd. She wasn't embarrassed talking about her feelings for Westley and the past connection that they'd, yet a simple suggestion of not accepting the invite to come to Hessleham Hall for the weekend had caused discomfort.

"Eddie asked me to come specifically. He wrote to me some weeks ago."

"How very odd."

"Odd indeed." Julia nodded her head in agreement. "One shouldn't speculate, but I couldn't help but imagine that his invitation meant he and Lillian were expecting and they wanted to ensure a place at my school for the infant."

"Do people really secure school placements for their children before they are even born?" Evelyn asked incredulously.

"They most certainly do," Julia said. "Particularly if it is an eminent school and they want to be absolutely positive their little darling will get a place."

"I think I always assumed Christie children got a place at your school because there was some sort of agreement."

Julia's eyes darkened. "There is."

Evelyn raised her eyebrows questioningly.

"It's called money," Julia snapped crossly, as though she hadn't wanted to say the words out loud.

"You're paid?"

"Charles called it a retainer. Something to do with an old agreement between him and my father."

Evelyn latched on to this new piece of information. "Your father knew Charles?"

"Yes, very well. They were at school together."

"So, in part, that is why you were invited this weekend?"

Julia shrugged. She didn't seem upset by Evelyn's questions. "It was actually Eddie who wrote and asked me to come, which is why I made the assumption about a potential heir. I don't know if he's aware of the arrangement between Charles and my father."

"And your father was not invited?"

Again, Julia gave Evelyn a strange, long look, as though she was determining how much Evelyn actually knew and the meaning behind what she was being asked. "My father would not come here again to this house for all the money in England. I, however, want to run a successful school and do not have the luxury of choice."

***

Tommy finally found Westley when Eddie was not monopolising his time. Though, on reflection, it seemed that finding Westley without a woman anywhere near him was the bigger miracle.

"I have spoken to the police and they are allowing us to shoot this afternoon," Tommy said as Westley shuffled papers on the desk in the library. "Do you shoot?"

"I'm not keen. I'm more of an indoor sports man." Westley shrugged. "But I shall, of course, join in."

"I wanted to ask you about the will," Tommy said. "About how the extra clause came to be added in."

"It's very simple," Westley's voice remained calm and measured, but Tommy sensed a stiffness in the other man's demeanour. "For some reason I was not privy to, Charles had become concerned about his mortality, but specifically that someone may want to kill him for financial gain."

"And would that include Lillian?"

Westley stopping rearranging paperwork and looked directly at Tommy for the first time. "Why would you ask that?"

Classic defection technique—reply to a question with another question. Had Westley forgotten Tommy's police background? "She was clearly frustrated that she had not received a bequest in Charles's will. This leads me to believe she had been told there was something in her favour. I don't know who she would have received that information from other than yourself or Charles."

"Not quite sure what you're asking me, old man." Westley's voice was now openly hostile.

"Did you tell Lillian she would receive money from Charles?"

"I did not."

"She was obviously expecting money, and this would have given her a motive to kill Charles." Tommy pointed out. "And you've just told me that Charles was worried, for some reason, and that someone wanted him dead. So, you can see why I'm asking about Lillian."

"What I can see is how you are trying to make some facts line up with others to fit your preconceived solution to Charles's death," Westley responded frostily.

According to Evelyn it was Eddie who had told Lillian she was going to inherit money in her own right. Was it possible Eddie had passed this information on to his wife hoping she would somehow engineer his father's death and create a win-win situation for the new Lord and Lady Northmoor? They were both certainly devious and selfish enough for that to be a genuine possibility.

"I thought perhaps your…um…affections for Lillian may have caused you…"

"My affections for Lillian?" Westley laughed uproariously. "I don't have affections for that woman!"

"Normally I wouldn't wish to be indiscrete," Tommy said. "But you were seen earlier today sharing a particularly personal moment with Lillian."

Westley opened his mouth and Tommy was certain words of denial would come forth, so he qualified his words. "Down by the river."

The solicitor was definitely squirming now, but Tommy couldn't be certain whether it was because he had been seen with Lillian or because proof of his feelings for Lillian were now out in the open.

Westley shrugged in a particularly careless way. "Lillian gets from me what she does not get from Eddie."

"Well, really!" Tommy exclaimed, though quite why he felt the need to attempt to defend Lillian's honour when she had been rude and nasty to everyone, he wasn't quite sure. "That's uncalled for."

"You're a man of the world," Westley sounded weary now. "Let's not make this conversation any more awkward than it already is."

"It is jolly awkward. Eddie is my cousin."

"And he prefers to run around the village after submissive young things who are flattered at the attentions of an older, wealthy man of a far superior social station." Westley held out his hands. "That leaves Lillian rather bored and in need of male attention."

"And you're only too happy to step in?" Tommy was frustrated with the other man's cavalier attitude. "It's a horrific conflict of interest as your job is supposed to be giving this family independent legal advice."

Westley pushed his chair back roughly and stood, his hands resting on the desk in front of him, his feet slightly apart as though he was ready to launch himself at Tommy. "Has anyone complained about my work?"

"They're hardly likely to," Tommy dropped his polite, indifferent attitude. Sometimes, and with some people, it really wasn't worth the effort. "The only person who could complain about the work you have done is dead, and the other senior members of my family have inherited his money and title."

"How dare you!"

The door banged open, and Eddie charged into the room. "What is going on in here? I can hear you arguing like schoolchildren in the corridor."

Given his behaviour the previous day, Tommy wasn't at all sure how Eddie dare make such a remark. Neither was he about to apologise for telling Westley that his conduct was unacceptable.

"Professional difference in opinion," Westley said smoothly, staring at Tommy and daring him to disagree with him.

Frustrated he couldn't tell Eddie what was going on without informing his cousin of his wife's infidelity, Tommy couldn't help leaving the room without firing one last shot. "It's true, there was a difference in opinion. But there was nothing professional about it."

Chapter Ten

After lunch, Tommy and Evelyn went upstairs to their bedroom to change clothes to prepare for the re-scheduled shoot.

"So, where do you think we are with this investigation?" Evelyn's frustrated tone matched Tommy's expression.

"I don't know, darling," he responded. "As you know, I appointed myself as liaison between the family and the police which they were most grateful for."

"Yes, I imagine so." Evelyn smiled, thinking most people would be relieved if they didn't have to deal with Eddie on a day-to-day basis.

"But investigation-wise, they seem to be as stumped as we are."

"Hmm," Evelyn grinned. "Rather like England were in the Ashes."

"Oh…oh…that's too far."

"It proves that I listen to you when you talk to me about cricket," Evelyn said airily. "I believe you told me it was the first time Australia won the series five to nil."

"I think I might prefer it if you don't listen to me," Tommy muttered.

Evelyn laughed. "So, did you get everything you wanted moved to the old smoking room?"

"I did." Tommy nodded. "Though, of course, the police are in there now. They don't seem to be showing any sign of moving out of the house anytime soon."

"I'm rather glad they're not," Evelyn said. "I feel rather unnerved by what's happened to Charles. At least whilst they are here nothing else will happen."

"You don't feel protected by me, your own husband?" Tommy asked, mock dismay on his face.

Evelyn smiled. "I always feel protected by you, darling, against dangers that we can see. Unfortunately, this poisoner has struck right at the very heart of the family."

"Yes," Tommy agreed. "It could be anyone. They could have laid the poison at literally any time. As we don't yet know how Charles was poisoned, we can't rule anyone out."

"You sound as frustrated as I am." Evelyn leaned her head against Tommy's shoulder. "Whatever are we to do next?"

"Would it help if we went through what we know, and what we would like to find out? That might help us work out the best way forward."

"Yes." Evelyn sat up and clapped her hands together. "A plan, that is exactly what we need to stop feeling so morose and ineffective."

"What do we need to find out?"

"We need to have a look around Charles' room. There may be nothing obvious, but apparently his valet says his medicine was missing. We need to check drawers and see if it was put in an unfamiliar place. We also need to check with Dr Mainwaring about what kind of medicine Charles was taking, and for what ailment."

"Yes." Tommy nodded in agreement. "That is one way the poison could potentially have been administered. Perhaps added to something that Charles regularly took? Perhaps he would not have noticed the bitter taste that Dr Mainwaring told me about if it was in medicine?"

"I will speak to Mrs Chapman and see if she noticed anything different in Charles' room. Or, actually, anyone else's, come to that."

"She knows everything."

"How long has she worked at Hessleham Hall?"

Tommy shrugged. "As long as I can remember. She hasn't changed one little bit over the years."

"She may well know what happened between Charles and Julia's father. Julia said enough to let me know that something happened and, whatever it was, her father would never come here again. I need to find out more."

"She's very stern. You'll have to be particularly charming."

"I have been told she is not very keen on Lillian." Evelyn lowered her voice, as if there was a chance of someone happening by their bedroom and listening outside the closed door. "So, I thought I would sympathise and lend her my support, given I'll soon be living here permanently."

"Oh, very well played, darling. That will appeal to her sense of proper order. She very much likes routine and for things to be done a certain way. I understand that Lillian has made that very difficult for her."

"Have you been talking to the staff too?"

"Brown sometimes tell me snippets of what is going on below stairs."

"Right." Evelyn nodded. "We also need to speak to Jack."

"I'll take care of that," Tommy said. "It would make sense as I am taking over the day to day running of the estate. I think I'll start by chatting to him amiably about the overabundance of rabbits at the village butcher's, assure him I'll be watching carefully, and then follow up by asking about Lillian. Hopefully, he'll be so concerned about keeping his job he'll tell me everything we need to know."

"That's very devious," Evelyn mused, head tilted to one side. "I think I like that side of you."

"And finally, I think we need to follow up with Oliver and Isobel about how and where they met. There's something going on there, I think."

"How very silly of me!" Evelyn exclaimed.

Tommy looked at her quizzically.

"Millicent worked at the hospital during the war. I shall simply give her a call and find out what she knows." Evelyn shook her head. "I can't believe I didn't think of that before now. And, of course, Reg is a doctor."

"Shall you telephone her?"

Evelyn wrinkled her nose. "On second thought, now the police are in the smoking room, I will send a note and then call on her in person."

It was practically impossible to have a private telephone call with anyone, given that the instrument was in the hallway and also it was so new, no one had yet learned to speak at a normal volume when using it.

"Are you happy with our plans?"

Evelyn nodded. She felt much better now she knew how they would progress their investigation of the crime. However, the terrible feeling of foreboding she'd felt after making bread in the kitchen had now increased, leaving her quite worried about what they would find out and whether that knowledge would affect their safety as Aunt Em had suggested.

***

"We may as well look at Charles' room now. We do have some time before the shoot starts," Tommy suggested.

Evelyn nodded and moved towards their bedroom door. "Is it odd that I feel rather nervous?"

Tommy caught hold of her hand. "Absolutely not, but we live here, and we are trying to get answers. We are not doing anything wrong."

"We're about to sneak around in a room that does not belong to us." Evelyn wrinkled her nose. "It's not right."

"I keep forgetting that I'm not doing this as a police officer," Tommy said. "If you're worried, I'll go by myself and report back."

"Not on your life," Evelyn retorted. "You're a man, you'll miss things that a woman's eye will see."

Evelyn couldn't hear Tommy's muttered response, but expected it was something along the lines of men being just as good at spotting things as women. She smiled as they made their way along the corridor, her hand firmly clutched in his—they may tease each other mercilessly, but there wasn't a thing they wouldn't do for each other.

"This next one." Tommy had moved to lead the way and indicated a door on the right.

Evelyn pulled in a deep breath, as though entering the room of a dead man would somehow infect her with the same poison as had killed him. She couldn't imagine that anything had much changed in the room since Charles changed for dinner less than forty-eight hours ago.

His day clothes still hung over the back of a chair near the window. Clearly his valet had not dared, or been allowed, to enter the room and complete his usual tasks following Charles' death. The bedding had been straightened but had not been made to the usual standards of the household—another sign that the staff had not been in the room since Charles had been taken out.

Evelyn swallowed over a lump in her throat at the sight of his slippers on the floor next to the left-hand side of his bed.

She didn't know why that insignificant thing affected her emotionally, but it did. The slippers sat waiting for feet that would never fill them. Charles hadn't even been a very pleasant man, but no one deserved to die before their time.

Tommy opened the wardrobe doors. "I'll start going through his clothes and see if there is anything in any of his pockets that may help us."

Evelyn nodded. "I'll do the same in his chest of drawers."

She moved over to the heavy walnut five drawer chest and started with the bottom drawer. Her heart thumped wildly in her chest. She wasn't sure whether it was excitement, fear or a horrid mixture of the two but whatever it was also made her feel a little nauseous. She wanted to find something that would help them discover who murdered Charles, yet she was also a little afraid of what would happen if they did.

The person they were hoping to uncover was either a family member or a person they saw regularly and knew well. She wasn't heeding Aunt Em's warning by staying away from the investigation, but she was at least starting to bear in mind the very real danger they could be putting themselves into by continuing their amateur sleuthing.

Finding nothing in any of the drawers, she moved over to the table beside Charles's bed. Kneeling next to his discarded slippers, she opened the single drawer of the bedside cabinet and gasped.

"What is it?" Tommy immediately stopped what he was doing and moved over to her side.

"His medicine," Evelyn answered in a voice that reflected the shock she was feeling. "His valet said it was missing."

"Don't touch it, the police will want to…" Tommy advised. "Oh dash!"

"What?"

"I will have to tell the police we've…I've been in here."

"Why would you need to do that?"

Tommy sighed. "If it wasn't there immediately after Charles's death, but now it's back, the police need to know. If it had already been put back before the police arrived, they also need to know it was reportedly missing before they arrived. It's my duty to make sure they have any information that could be crucial. I believe they will want to see if they can get any fingerprints from the bottle."

Evelyn lay a hand on his back. "How will you explain what we were doing in here?"

Tommy lifted a shoulder. "I don't know. I must think of something plausible."

"Is it possible you could suggest to the police you were looking for something you need for the shoot, perhaps that you leant to Charles, but now need back?"

"I guess that's as good a reason for me to be in here as any," Tommy said. "I don't have any other excuse that I can think of."

They completed the rest of their search in silence, Evelyn worried for Tommy. The police had refused to allow him to help their investigations, despite his experience and exemplary record both in the police force and whilst he was in the Army. She understood why that was, she really did, but in her mind, they couldn't have anyone finer assisting them.

Then there had been that unfortunate argument between Tommy and Eddie after lunch the previous day, which someone would have been sure to tell the police all about. Tommy hadn't mentioned to her they had questioned him about the incident, but that would be just like him—he wouldn't want her to worry.

And now he had to go admit to snooping in Charles' room. However plausible his explanation may be, it would look exactly like it was—he was prying into things and places where he had no business being. She hadn't missed how he'd changed his wording either. He would not tell the police that she had been right there by his side. He would simply confess to his own presence.

"Anything else?" Tommy asked eventually, his voice sounding as defeated as she felt.

"No." Evelyn shook her head. "Nothing more. I've looked under the bed and felt underneath the mattress."

"Righto," Tommy said. "You go with Nancy to meet the others and I will speak to the police."

They exited the room and Evelyn paused outside of theirs. Tommy walked away from her down the corridor, back straight and his steps measured and precise. She knew that was a style he had developed so that no extra pressure was put on the leg he had injured during the war, rather than a military gait that marked him as the soldier he had been.

Evelyn made herself focus on the shoot, and what she had to do to get herself and Nancy prepared, and less on how the police would take Tommy's confession in the light of the terrible events of the last few days.

Chapter Eleven

Tommy left the old smoking room and headed outside. He had been sternly rebuked, and it left him feeling absolutely dreadful. It reminded him of being a child when his father had been displeased with him. There had been no shouting, no threats of liberties being removed, just a cold and steely censure of his behaviour that left him feeling as though he hadn't lived up to expectations and had let down his entire family.

He would never, ever allow a child of his to feel that way.

That one simple thought lightened his step and put a smile back on his face. The very idea of his and Evelyn's child always raised his spirits. Not that he had persuaded Evelyn as to what an immensely marvellous idea it was. She had not only been dissuaded from rushing to be a mother by her own childhood but also by the relentless pressure for an heir produced by families such as his own.

Times had changed and his wife was definitely not a submissive creature, but a partner who constantly challenged him to be a better man simply by her sweet yet spirited nature.

He caught sight of her walking ahead, Nancy at her side, talking animatedly with Julia Davenport. The other woman was much taller than Evelyn, yet his wife kept pace as they moved towards where the shoot would begin.

Tommy looked around and located Jack Partridge, who was towards the head of the group. He hurried to catch up, passing Evelyn on his way.

"Mr Christie, sir," Jack said as Tommy reached his side.

"Partridge." Tommy nodded in acknowledgement. "Are you thankful this season's shooting is about to begin at last?"

"Not quite as thankful as Mr Eddie." Jack flushed. "That is…the Earl of Northmoor. He has been so very keen to not miss another day of the season."

"Indeed," Tommy murmured, aware by Jack's reaction to his slip that Eddie was already an absolute slave to propriety. "Eddie is a very keen sportsman."

Privately, though, Tommy wondered why his cousin was quite as keen on shooting as he was, given he was such a terrible shot. Usually one enjoyed something one was particularly good at and did not like doing things one performed poorly. But then Eddie had married the girl who, it was claimed, was the prettiest girl in the north and then proceeded to more or less ignore her.

Of course, it was all about image with Eddie—he must shoot this weekend because people would talk if he didn't; he must have the most beautiful wife, even if he did not love her. Not for the first time, Tommy considered what would happen if Eddie did not produce an heir. It certainly seemed from what he and Evelyn had learned that Eddie and Lillian were as unfaithful as each other—though that had been before the death of Charles. Surely everything would be different now?

"Very keen indeed, Mr Christie." Jack agreed.

"Has the earl told you of his plans for me to run the estate for him?" Tommy asked. "Of course, you are to remain the estate manager, but I am to work closely with you and ensure you have everything you need in order to do your job properly."

"That's very kind," Jack said, his words simple, but the look behind his eyes anything but. "It will be very useful to have some extra help and support."

"Speaking of which," Tommy said smoothly. "Is there anything you can think of immediately that you need help with? Maybe some extra staff to help keep poachers off the land? That kind of thing? I know my uncle wasn't keen to spend money, and so it could be you've needed extra help before, but we have refused it?"

Tommy feared he'd rather over-egged the pudding with his brief speech. He loved his wife, but sounding like her when he spoke by using too many words was not a positive thing. Men should speak only when they had something to say, and then they should stick to the words necessary to make their point and not use any extra. Women, however, could use as many as they liked. These behavioural norms kept a proper conversational balance.

"I hadn't really thought about it," Jack mumbled, looking everywhere but directly at Tommy.

"Well, old chap," Tommy said. "Please do think about it and let me have an answer by morning."

That was certainly short and to the point, Tommy was quite proud of the self-assurance and authority in his tone. When dealing with other people, being polite and fair would always come first with him, but he needed to work more on his leadership qualities. Since the war, he had had little cause to, but if he was going to run the estate successfully, he needed to ensure he was not seen as a soft touch.

"Well," Jack paused, seemingly stunned by Tommy's words. "Of course."

"The other thing I wanted to talk to you about is a little bit more…um…" Tommy searched for the right word. "Personal."

If the other man had seemed uncomfortable before, now he looked like he wanted to run and never look back. "Sir?"

"It has come to my attention that you have been involved with my sister-in-law in some sort of friendship."

"What?" Jack spluttered. "Who has told you such a thing? I'll...I'll kill whoever…"

"Now, now." Tommy held up a hand. "Hardly the right choice of words at this time, let alone whilst you have a gun in your hands."

"Yes, sorry, Mr Christie," Jack said, chastened. Then he looked up at Tommy, fury in his eyes. "But who told you that?"

"The lady herself," Tommy said smoothly. "Not directly to me, but to my wife."

"Lillian said that to Mrs Christie?" Jack repeated hoarsely, then shook his head. "Well, I never."

Tommy nodded. "What do you have to say for yourself?"

Jack shook his head, and for a moment, Tommy thought he would deny it. "I have nothing to say."

"It is true, then?"

Jack nodded.

"Well, this puts me in a tough position," Tommy told him. "I'm to work closely with you regarding the estate and particularly with the problem we have with poachers and you're involved with Lady Northmoor."

"Was," Jack told him. "Was involved."

"You have ended the…liaison?"

"Actually, she…Lillian…um…Lady Northmoor just stopped coming around."

"What do you mean?" Tommy was getting quite frustrated by the conversation. Of course, it was difficult for the other man, given his position, but all he wanted was to get to the truth and then they could never talk about such a personal topic ever again.

"Lady Northmoor…she would come to my cottage. Now she doesn't."

Tommy knew that Jack had a cottage on the estate grounds, as did a few other employees. He could scarcely believe that Lillian had been so brazen as to visit Jack's home. "Why would she think she could do such a thing?"

Jack shook his head, a miserable look on his face. "She's always walking around the grounds, finding out what she can, then using the information to get what she wants."

Tommy stopped walking and grabbed hold of Jack's arm. "Can we please just talk plainly?"

"I don't want to lose my job."

"Then tell me everything, right now, and I can assure you that you will not."

"The poaching," Jack began, his face bright red. "I know you've worked it out. Lillian caught me one day and after that, she started visiting me. How could I turn her away?"

"Because of who she was and also what she knew?"

Jack nodded, staring off into the distance. "It was such a relief when she stopped turning up."

"I'm sure," Tommy agreed, thinking what a thoroughly nasty piece of work his sister-in-law was. "Right, we shall say no more about it. Tomorrow we will start our working relationship as though today never happened."

"I would be ever so grateful, sir."

Tommy breathed in a deep lungful of clean air, thankful that particular conversation was over and done with. It seemed his job wouldn't just be to keep an eye on the running of the estate, but also on the people who lived and worked there. He was exhausted just thinking about it.

Only when Evelyn caught up with him did he remember he had forgotten to ask Jack where he had gone when Charles fell ill.

***

"Ah, Mrs Chapman. I have been looking for you," Evelyn said as she found the housekeeper on the landing near Charles' room. The woman looked incredibly nervous. "Is there something wrong?"

"Of course not, Mrs Christie." Mrs Chapman said very smoothly. "I have simply been locking up the old earl's room, as requested by the police."

"Ah..." Evelyn gathered herself, aware she herself now sounded rather wary. "I fear that may be my fault."

"Yes," Mrs Chapman agreed. "I had heard that."

For a moment, Evelyn was taken back by the woman's honesty. Usually staff were more reticent when they spoke to her. "May we speak in my room?"

"In your room?" Mrs Chapman frowned.

"I would not want our conversation to be overheard." Evelyn lowered her voice and looked along the corridor, as though there were people everywhere—there was actually no one else in sight. "I would hate for Lady Northmoor to see us talking."

"Very well." Mrs Chapman nodded her agreement. Mrs O'Connell had been quite correct. A single mention of Lillian and Mrs Chapman's demeanour had changed immediately.

"Thank you for talking to me," Evelyn said, as soon as they were inside her room. They both knew there hadn't been a decision to make. As Evelyn was a member of the family and the housekeeper a member of staff—there was no actual choice. "Since my husband and I have been staying here, we've noticed a number of things that have concerned us greatly."

"Have we not looked after you to your liking?" Mrs Chapman asked sharply.

"Oh, on the contrary." Evelyn smiled. "We have been looked after quite beautifully. Your staff are to be commended. Please do pass on my highest compliments to them, as a guest of course. It's not at all my intention to undermine Lady Northmoor."

Mrs Chapman's lips twitched, as though she was well aware of what Evelyn was doing. "I shall let them know, thank you."

"I understand that you have worked here for many years. Mr Christie tells me you've been here for as long as he can remember."

Mrs Chapman smiled then, as though recalling something particularly pleasant. "Yes, I remember young Mr Tommy coming here as an infant with his parents."

"I expect that means you know everything about everyone that has ever stayed here."

"I expect it does," Mrs Chapman agreed. "However, that doesn't mean that I will share that knowledge with you. A very large, and important, part of my job is to be discrete, Mrs Christie."

"I understand." Evelyn nodded. "However, I am very concerned about the safety of everyone is in the house whilst a murderer runs unchallenged amongst us."

"With all due respect," Mrs Chapman said. "I believe that is why the police are here."

"And what have they done so far?" Evelyn challenged. "To my mind, not very much. For instance, they do not know about Lord and Lady Northmoor's penchant for liaisons outside of their marriage."

Mrs Chapman's eyebrows shot upwards at Evelyn's words. "Well, I wouldn't…"

Evelyn held up a hand. "I understand, Mrs Chapman. It is not a proper conversation for us to have."

"And yet we seem to be having it," she retorted.

"We must," Evelyn insisted. "As I said, I am concerned that there is some knowledge that you may have that can help Mr Christie and I to identify the culprit."

"I really do think you should leave investigating to the police."

"As you are no doubt aware, Mr Christie is the police," Evelyn said in a sharp voice. She needed this woman's help, not a diatribe on what she should and should not be doing.

Mrs Chapman's pulled her face into an emotional mask, hiding the sceptical look that had followed Evelyn's words. Of course, Mrs Chapman was right to look dubious, as Tommy wasn't actually the police. Not anymore. "How can I help you, Mrs Christie?"

"As I said," Evelyn hurried her words, wanting to say all she needed to so she could convince Mrs Chapman to be honest with her. "Mr Christie and I know that there have been several extra-marital affairs within the household which may, or may not, have something to do with the previous earl's death. It also seems that everyone here is hiding something. All we wish to do is get to the bottom of everything, pass what we know on to the police, and let them apprehend the murderer."

"If I can help, I will, but I can't think I know something that will assist."

"What do you know about the vicar and his wife?"

Mrs Chapman shook her head. "Absolutely nothing."

"There was nothing between Mrs Turnbull and Charles?"

"Oh, my goodness, no."

"You seem very certain."

"I sometimes hear gossip that I pay no attention to. But regarding anyone being involved with the old earl, I have never heard a single thing."

"We can strike that off our list." Evelyn nodded in satisfaction. "The other person who has me quite perplexed is Julia Davenport. I understand her father and Charles were friendly?"

"Herbert Davenport visited Hessleham Hall frequently," Mrs Chapman confirmed.

"Until when?"

"I can't exactly remember how many years it has been." Mrs Chapman wrinkled her brow in deep concentration. "But I can recall precisely what it was that stopped him returning."

"That would be very useful."

"It was a game of cards," Mrs Chapman said. "It went on and on. Malton and the footman at the time thought they would not get to bed before they had to be up to serve breakfast."

"Goodness," Evelyn murmured.

"Anyway," Mrs Chapman continued. "You don't want to know about all of that. You need to know what it was that happened at the end of the card game."

"Quite."

"Mr Davenport had wagered the school on his hand of cards," Mrs Chapman paused before confiding. "And he lost."

"Charles won the hand and as a result then owned Mr Davenport's school?"

"That is correct." Mrs Chapman nodded. "But that is not all."

"It isn't?"

"Malton heard everything, and he told me that Mr Charles and Mr Eddie discussed inviting Miss Davenport here this weekend."

"Really?" Evelyn wanted to hurry the woman up. Now she had started talking, she didn't seem to want to stop, but Evelyn was sure there was a juicy piece of information coming up and she was eager to hear it right away.

"It seems there's a child in the village that Mr Eddie wanted admitted to the school. With no fees being due from that child's parents."

"What would that have to do with Eddie?" Evelyn was confused.

"Well, it's very delicate," Mrs Chapman said. "But you have asked me what I know."

"Indeed, yes," Evelyn nodded. "Do carry on, I can assure you that nothing you can tell me will trouble my sensibilities, such as they are."

"The child is Eddie's son."

Evelyn covered her mouth with one hand. She had not expected that. "And he wants Miss Davenport to educate him?"

"Yes, and without payment," Mrs Chapman confirmed. "Which she cannot argue with as her family no longer owns the school. The old earl does...well I expect that means the current Earl of Northmoor now owns the school, so the decision is quite out of Miss Davenport's hands."

"I wonder, does Miss Davenport receive a wage?"

"I couldn't say what the arrangements are." Mrs Chapman held out her hands. "I only know that the Davenports lost the school in a poor bet and that Miss Davenport has been asked here this weekend specifically to discuss the child."

"Thank you, Mrs Chapman. You've been very helpful."

The housekeeper nodded and left the room, leaving Evelyn more confused than ever. Julia was being asked to do something that she, no doubt, felt ethically was very wrong. However, because she had no control over the school, there was nothing she could do but comply.

Was that a strong enough motive for murder? Would Julia believe that with Charles out of the way, she could get the school back? As a teacher, would she know anything about poisons?

With so many more questions than she had before. She would need to speak to Julia again.

Chapter Twelve

After she had spoken to Mrs Chapman and the rest of the party had finished afternoon tea, they headed back outside to carry on the shoot. Westley Harrison, it turned out, had been telling the truth, at least about his prowess with a gun. He was a remarkably bad shot. If there had been a contest between Eddie and Westley for the very worst, it would have been a close-run thing.

Lillian had stayed home with Aunt Em, though Evelyn doubted they would be spending any time in each other's company, so she had asked Doris to keep a discrete eye on Lillian's movements whilst they were out.

Oliver and Isobel trudged along together, neither of them looking much as though they wanted to be there—either at the shoot or anywhere together.

Dr Mainwaring had paired up with Julia, which left Jack as the odd man out, but he didn't seem to mind. After his discussion with Tommy earlier, it wasn't a surprise to Evelyn that Jack kept himself to himself and did not try to engage anyone in conversation.

Evelyn and Tommy always worked with Nancy. Of course, there were other estate dogs that were taken out on the shoot, but Evelyn particularly preferred to only work with the dog she had trained herself. She trusted Nancy in a way that she didn't think she would trust one of the other animals.

The moorland to the east of the house was perfect for grouse shooting. Nancy was excellent at hunting game and then waiting for Evelyn to approach. At her command, the dog would flush out the birds, giving Evelyn and Tommy an opportunity to shoot. Nancy didn't seem to enjoy retrieving, which Evelyn could completely understand, but she had trained her to do all three necessary components and so was a good all-round gundog.

They walked along the path through the middle of the lawn and through a gate into the moor beyond. Nancy ran on in front of them, dancing in a crazy circle and then returning, excited to be free again in the open air for the second time that day. Evelyn had told Tommy what Mrs Chapman had said about Julia and her family, and it all confused him as much as it did her.

"Oh goodness," Evelyn said under her breath. "Do you think that's how Julia came to know Westley Harrison? Perhaps she went to ask his professional opinion about the legality of the card game?"

"And then they fell in love?" Tommy raised an eyebrow.

"I don't think there was any love involved," Evelyn said. "At least not on Westley's part. Julia certainly seemed upset that he had moved on, though."

"It would make sense as to a meeting. I must admit, darling, I'm very irritated about what I've learned about my family these last couple of days. They don't seem to have a moral compass between them."

"It makes me feel very lucky that I have you." Evelyn linked her arm through Tommy's. "You have enough moral fibre for the entire family, luckily for me."

Within minutes, Eddie gave the command for the shoot to get underway. The dogs started locating grouse, and the shooting began. The sound and smell of gunfire filled the air alongside the excited barking of the dogs.

As the afternoon wore on and became early evening, the participants had spread out across the moor and Evelyn had grown bored. She liked to show off her dog and particularly Nancy's capabilities, but she herself wasn't competitive regarding how many grouse she had shot compared to anyone else.

Evelyn hung back, leaving Tommy in front with Nancy. Her mind wasn't really on the shoot. It was still on the mixed muddle of clues and information they had gathered—none of which made any sense or seemed to fit together.

She was thinking about going back to the house when a sudden shout went up together with a scream that tore through the air. Panicked, Evelyn ran towards the sound of the uproar, and where their group stood in a haphazard circle. Her feet slipped over the uneven ground in her haste to see what had happened.

Approaching everyone, she tried to catch her breath. "What is it? What has happened?"

"It's Eddie." Oliver Turnbull turned away from the figure Evelyn could now see laying prostrate on the rough carpet of moorland. "He's been shot."

"Shot?" Evelyn echoed. "But how could that happen?"

"It must have been a terrible accident," Isobel said firmly, calmer than Evelyn had ever seen her. "That's the only explanation."

She nodded, the shock of seeing Eddie on the floor with blood spreading out in a red stain across his white shirt, leaving her completely speechless.

"Don't look, darling." Tommy turned her away from the awful sight and wrapped his arms around her.

"What happened?"

"I didn't see." Evelyn felt Tommy shrug against her. "I just didn't see. We had spread out, and we were all shooting from different directions. I don't know how it could have happened."

She could feel him trembling against her and knew that whilst the sound of shooting didn't remind him of his awful days serving his country throughout the Great War, the sight of a man bleeding on the ground certainly had done so.

They held onto each other tightly, both giving and receiving comfort.

It was long moments before the full enormity of what had happened hit Evelyn.

Eddie was dead.

Astonishingly, that meant she and Tommy had just become Lord and Lady Northmoor.

***

The police met them at the side door to the house, having been alerted by Jack Partridge who had run back up to the house. They had left Dr Mainwaring with the body. Not because there was a single thing the man could do for Eddie, but because it was not right to leave him lying on the moor all alone.

"What happened?" Detective Inspector Andrews, the most senior of the two policemen, addressed Tommy directly. "How could this have happened?"

"An accident," Isobel said, repeating what she had said directly after the incident.

"Wait in the drawing room," the detective said, then to his colleague: "Go with them and stay with them. I need to call for backup."

Malton and Mrs Chapman stood off to the side, their usually carefully arranged features horrified. Evelyn herself was shocked. Her legs trembled, and she felt as though if she didn't sit down soon, she would fall.

"Can we have tea in the drawing room, please?" she asked. "And something light to eat. Perhaps some sandwiches, if Mrs O'Connell has the time."

"Very good," Mrs Chapman paused, caught herself, then continued. "My Lady."

Evelyn flushed. She hadn't made the request because she was 'lady of the house' but because she herself felt in need of refreshments and thought everyone else probably did too—regardless of the fact the household had officially already had afternoon tea once that day. Lillian would have to be told the news, and Evelyn needed to keep up her strength to deal with her sister-in-law.

Aunt Em was already seated in the drawing room as the dumbstruck group began to slowly trail along the corridor and into the room. The old lady rose as they came in and walked up to Evelyn. "My dear, what a terrible shock. How are you?"

Evelyn nodded. It would be poor form to pretend to be grief-stricken because, of course, she wasn't. She hadn't liked Eddie at all. "What happened was very distressing. It was an appalling thing to see. Where is Lillian?"

Aunt Em shook her head. "I don't know."

"Is she aware of what has happened?"

"I do not believe so."

At that moment, a knock sounded at the door. The police detective opened it to reveal Doris standing on the other side, looking petrified. She looked around the room and settled on Evelyn who hurried over to where the girl stood.

"Doris?"

"Mrs Christie, you asked me to watch Lillian," Doris whispered. "She sat in here for a time after you had all left and then became unwell."

"Unwell?" Evelyn considered this for a moment. "It's all right, Doris. Do not worry about what you're saying. Just tell me the truth as it is."

Doris nodded. "Agnes had to help her upstairs because she was absolutely sozzled. I believe she's still in her room."

"Thank you very much," Evelyn said. "You've been very helpful."

Doris bobbed her head. "Shall I take Nancy?"

Evelyn had been so upset by what happened, she had not realised Nancy had faithfully trotted at her side and now lay next to the sofa where she had been sitting before getting up to speak to Doris. "No, thank you, Doris. If you don't mind, I think I would rather like to keep her close to me."

Doris left the room, and Evelyn turned to the detective. "You heard the conversation, I'm sure. No doubt your colleague will want to check on Mrs Christie, and someone will have to break the awful news to her."

"Yes, ma'am," he replied.

"My Lady!" Aunt Em barked.

"I...what?" He responded, a perplexed look on his face.

"When you address Lady Northmoor." Aunt Em indicated Evelyn to illustrate her point. "It should be as 'My Lady' and most definitely not ma'am."

"Aunt Em, really, these things do not matter right now."

"They most certainly do," Aunt Em disagreed. "My dear, they matter now more than ever. If we forget propriety, wherever will we end up?"

Evelyn didn't have an answer to that. She did, however, have an awfully funny feeling in her stomach. It was as though someone was squeezing her insides. The feeling spread upwards and prevented her from taking a deep breath. The only other time she could recall such a horrid sensation was when she was told Tommy had been injured during the war and she was not aware of the severity of his injuries.

She sat back on the sofa and clasped her hands together. She needed to get a hold of herself. Aunt Em was correct in that she now had a particular position. Whether she wanted that position was not relevant. Reaching out, she stroked the top of Nancy's head. The dog had leaned against the sofa as though she knew her mistress would need the comfort of laying her hand on the dog's warm fur.

The door crashed open, nearly knocking over the detective who leaned against it. He stumbled, righted himself, and glared at the person who had roughly shoved their way into the room.

"I have heard the news!" Lillian's announcement was loud, her voice showing no trace of any emotion other than a touch of anger.

Her hair and make-up were perfect, as though she had taken the time to ensure she looked nothing short of spectacular before returning downstairs.

Evelyn stood and walked over to her. "May I offer my sympathies, what a dreadful…"

"Oh, do stop!" Lillian screeched, holding out her arms so Evelyn could not get close to her. "You didn't like him. None of you *liked* him!"

"Well, as that may be," Evelyn intoned calmly. "However, what's happened has been a dreadful shock for everyone."

"Begging your pardon, My Lady," Malton said imperiously from the doorway. "But might now be a good time to serve tea?"

Lillian whirled around. "We have already had afternoon tea. I do not understand this English fascination to force tea on people every time there is a crisis. I do not want any more of the stuff!"

If Lillian's dramatics offended or upset Malton, it did not show on his face. However, he made no move to enter the room with the tea tray but stood looking at Evelyn.

"Thank you, Malton, now would be a perfect time for tea." Evelyn smiled.

"Very good, My Lady." He entered the room, followed by one of the maids who carried a large silver salver containing delicate sandwiches with various different fillings.

Lillian stared between Malton and Evelyn, and for one awful moment, Evelyn feared she would attack the butler and knock the tray from his hands.

"Of course." She sneered at Evelyn. "I am not surprised to find you are playing lady of the manor already."

The maid looked terrified as she followed Malton and placed the large tray on a side table. Evelyn wanted to tell Lillian the truth, that she had asked for the refreshments because she herself felt in need, but instead she recalled Aunt Em's words.

"I am not playing anything, Lillian," Evelyn stared directly at Lillian and did not back down, even though inside she was quivering with fear that the other woman could strike her at any moment. She wished she'd moved away from Lillian before speaking. "I have had no control over events. Circumstances have now come about, however, meaning I am now Lady Northmoor."

She could have added 'whether or not I like it' but that would show a weakness Lillian would immediately pounce on and take advantage of.

"Circumstances?" Lillian screeched. "Circumstances have not brought about my Eddie's untimely death!"

"Perhaps you might sit down and have a drink?" Evelyn suggested quietly.

"You!" Lillian pointed, reaching out so her finger jabbed Evelyn in the chest. "You and your husband have made this happen. Only yesterday your darling Tommy threatened Eddie in front of everyone. Mark my words, I will see him hang for this!"

With those dramatic words, she turned and flounced out of the room.

Evelyn breathed past the lump in her throat and walked over to the table. "Tea everyone? I shall pour."

Aunt Em clapped her hands together once. "Absolutely magnificent!"

Evelyn smiled, certain that Aunt Em was not referring to the tea.

Chapter Thirteen

The next morning, Evelyn spoke to Detective Inspector Andrews to ensure she could leave the house and visit her sister Millicent as planned. As soon as they granted permission, she took Nancy with her and refused all offers of a lift.

Malton stood at the doorway of the house, flanked by two uniformed police officers and shaking his head in disbelief at her decision. He had told her several times it would be much more appropriate for her to allow him to get the car brought around for her, but she had refused.

She wanted to walk into the village, and needed the time alone to clear her head and organise her thoughts. For once, since the death of Charles, her mind wasn't occupied by thoughts of murder and mayhem. Instead, she needed to make some sort of sense of her new position. The last few days had a surreal feeling around them which Evelyn thought would likely last for some time.

Millicent, Evelyn's sister, opened the door to her house before Evelyn raised the brass knocker. "Evelyn! Come in!"

Milly did everything faster, quicker and better than anyone Evelyn had ever met. Whilst their mother's slapdash parenting style had made Evelyn quiet, contemplative and a little unsure of herself, it had made Milly an absolute paragon of perfection.

Evelyn reached forward and kissed her sister's cheek. "Morning, Milly."

Milly held a hand up to her mouth in a gesture of mock horror. "Do I have to curtsy or something?"

Evelyn flapped her elder sister's hand away. "Don't be silly. Of course not."

"I simply could not believe it when I heard," Milly went on, leading the way into her compact drawing room. "Ethel has taken the children out so we can talk in peace."

Evelyn nodded, glad they could talk, but unusually missing their boisterous presence. Normally she seemed to leave Milly's house with a headache. Today, she longed for their noise and total enthusiasm for everything.

"It has been dreadful."

"You poor darling," her sister sympathised. "Sit down, I already have a tray prepared. I knew you wouldn't be late."

The note she had sent to her sister had promised she would call at ten that morning. Whilst their mother wouldn't think twice of sending a similar note, in reality it meant she might call, should she remember. Evelyn would not do that to Milly. Her sister's life was ordered, and everything ran in perfect synchronisation. Milly's house was the absolute opposite to the one they had been raised in, and Evelyn respected her sister's right to that structure.

"How did you hear?"

Milly smiled. "The butcher's boy is sweet on one of your kitchen maids. She told him yesterday afternoon when he was delivering sausages for Nancy. The entire village knew about Eddie before a single evening meal was served."

"Goodness." Evelyn nodded. "I was aware news travelled fast in this village, but that is quick. And I fear Nancy will look like a sausage if Albert keeps using that as an excuse to visit Nora."

The dog thumped her tail at the mention of her name.

"He's a very nice boy," Milly said, pouring coffee into two delicate blue-patterned china cups. "I know his mother."

Of course she did. There wasn't a person in the village Milly did not know. Most of them had been cajoled, or downright bullied, by Milly at one time or another to perform some duty or provide some service for Milly's newest cause. There wasn't a time that her sister wasn't doing something to help others.

Evelyn took the saucer from her sister and rested it in her lap. "So, about the vicar and his wife?"

"I didn't remember either of them," Milly said. "However, I spoke to Reg about the Turnbulls and he remembers Oliver very well."

"From the hospital?"

"Yes, before the war." Milly nodded. "It was dreadful. *Quite* the scandal. I cannot believe I didn't recall the details until Reg reminded me."

"There was a scandal?"

"Yes, it was absolutely dreadful."

"But no one in the village remembers this?"

"Well, of course," Milly reminded Evelyn. "Neither Oliver nor Isobel came from Hessleham, though they have lived here for some years now. The gossip would have circulated around where they lived at the time, which is, no doubt, the reason they moved here. For a fresh start."

"Whatever did they do?"

"Fell in love," Milly said simply. "Madly in love, Reg says."

"And that was scandalous?"

Milly nodded. "Oh, it absolutely was because, you see, Oliver was married to someone else."

"Goodness." Evelyn took a sip of tea and sighed. "Is absolutely everyone unfaithful these days?"

"Not everyone I shouldn't think," Milly said matter of factly. "But in villages, it's just less easy to hide. And, of course, a hospital is like a village in that everyone knows everyone, and nothing is kept as secret as some may like."

"What happened to Oliver's wife?"

"Well, that's the truly scandalous part," Milly said, leaning forward towards Evelyn, as she got to the meat of her story. "Oliver's wife was in the hospital. Something about having had an accident, and she had been in a coma practically forever."

"How very sad," Evelyn murmured.

"Indeed." Milly nodded. "But then Oliver met and fell in love with Isobel. And even though his poor wife had been in a coma for ages, within weeks of the affair beginning, Oliver's wife suddenly upped and died."

Evelyn gasped. "And people assumed either Oliver or Isobel had something to do with her death?"

"Reg says simply *everyone* believed someone finished the poor woman off so Oliver and Isobel could be together."

"Did Oliver work at the hospital? Is that how they met?"

"Oh, no." Milly shook her head emphatically. "He wasn't even a vicar then. They met as he was always there visiting his wife. Apparently, he spent hours sitting by her bedside holding her hand."

"That's just heart-breaking." Evelyn shuddered and remembered when she had not received a letter for weeks from Tommy and didn't know if he was lying on a field somewhere in France injured or if he was actually dead. She couldn't imagine falling in love with someone else during that uncertain time, let alone becoming involved with someone else whilst he was still alive.

"Does that information help at all?"

"Well," Evelyn said, finishing her tea and putting the saucer on the side table. "It's rather like everything else I have found out since Charles died. It explains some things but raises still more questions."

"You do know," Milly said clasping her hands together in her lap, a serious look on her face. "That some things are better off remaining in the past, and shouldn't be interfered with?"

"Do you really believe that?" Evelyn asked, surprised. Her sister had always been such a stickler for the truth and for everything to be so very perfect.

"Yes," Milly said firmly. "I very much do. And further, it could be dangerous if you go poking your nose into places where it doesn't belong."

"Aunt Em said something quite similar."

"Well, then." Milly clapped her hands together. "Then it seems you should listen to the two wisest women in your life and concentrate on your new life as Lady Northmoor. I shall need your help in organising the village fete shortly."

"Milly!" Evelyn exclaimed. "They always hold the village fete in July, and it's now August."

"Ah." Milly nodded. "But Lillian wouldn't allow us to have the fete on the grounds of Hessleham Hall as we usually do, so we had to cancel it."

"That wasn't really Lillian's decision to make, was it?"

"We both know that Charles wasn't at all interested in the village or in our traditions and was probably quite happy with Lillian's decision should he have been aware of it." Milly got to her feet. "But now, my dearest sister, I know I shall be able to count on your support."

Evelyn had hoped the walk to Milly's home would clear her mind, but she left feeling even more befuddled. The news regarding Oliver and Isobel Turnbull had confused her. It made sense that Isobel remembered meeting Oliver as a happy time because falling in love was very exciting, but then refused to say more because the only way they had been able to marry was due to Oliver's first wife dying. That wasn't the sort of thing one would want to discuss.

And now her sister was very definitely going to be relying on her to use her influence as Lady Northmoor—Evelyn finally accepted that the quiet life she and Tommy had been enjoying since the war was most definitely over.

Things would never be quite the same ever again.

***

Evelyn walked back through the village and to the lane that led to the manor, her tread heavier and much slower than on the way to Milly's house. She would miss her cottage in the village. It had been the first home she had shared with Tommy and where she had lived those lonely years without him whilst he had served his country. It was also where she had helped nurse him back to health when he returned from France with such a terrible leg injury.

They had lived there very happily with just Doris and a lady from the village who came in three times a week to cook meals. Of course, she would only live a brief walk away in the manor, but in many respects, she may as well be on a different continent.

She would have additional responsibilities and duties as Lady Northmoor, probably more than she could even imagine as it had been so many years since anyone had held that role. She expected to receive lots of correspondence over the next few weeks.

Malton's face as he opened the door for her upon her return was as white as it had been the afternoon before when they had returned to the house following Eddie's death. He nodded. "Lady Northmoor."

"Malton," she replied. "Are you feeling unwell?"

"I'm afraid there have been some developments since you left for the village."

Developments? Surely there couldn't have been another death. Her breath caught in her throat as she tried to look past Malton into the house. She gasped and her hand flew to cover her mouth. "Where's Tommy?"

"I'm afraid that's what I was trying to tell you," Malton said with a definite quiver in his voice. "They have arrested Lord Northmoor."

"Arrested?" Evelyn repeated. "Whatever do you mean?"

"It's exactly as it sounds," Detective Inspector Andrews said as he came out of the old smoking room. "We have arrested your husband. He is currently being taken to York for further questioning."

Evelyn drew herself up to her full height, which sadly did not make her very imposing at just over five foot. She was angrier than she had ever been in her entire life.

This was worse than her mother missing her perfect performance as Mary in the school nativity performance, more frustrating than her mother forgetting completely to turn up to Evelyn's twenty-first birthday celebrations and infinitively more dreadful than her mother rushing into the church late for Evelyn's wedding.

"Did he really have to be taken to York?" Evelyn hardly recognised her own voice. Gone was the hesitant, slightly embarrassed tone she was aware was prevalent in her voice when dealing with people she was unsure of. Following the developments of the last few days, it was almost as though she had suddenly become a real grownup. "Why could you not ask him the questions you needed answers to here in the house? That would surely have afforded him the dignity he deserves?"

The detective flushed a very unbecoming red that started directly above the white collar of his shirt and rushed up into his cheeks at Evelyn's unwavering stare. "Well…it's like this…"

Evelyn had had quite enough of this house, the people in it, and everything that had happened over the last few days. She felt her last ounce of self-control snap. "Speak up, man!"

Her voice echoed along the corridor. Only a couple of hours earlier, she would have cringed at the sound of her own voice talking to someone in such a curt manner. Now she found she was actually jolly proud of herself.

"Lady Northmoor said…that is…"

"I believe what the detective is trying to tell you." Malton stepped forward. He now seemed quite recovered. "Is that the Dowager Countess, Mrs Lillian Christie, was very insistent in her belief that Lord Northmoor killed her husband because of their slight disagreement after the death of the fifth Earl of Northmoor. She said Lord Northmoor must be removed from the house immediately because she did not feel safe with him under the same roof. She went on to say she believed that the detectives' superiors would be interested to hear of their 'terrible handling' of matters so far."

Evelyn's head swam at the changes in the family lineage over the last few days. She noticed that the detective appeared even more confused than her and looked as though he would rather be anywhere else but standing in the hall of the manor house under her increasingly furious glare.

"Let me see if I have this correct," Evelyn said, her voice low and clear. "Whilst I have been away from the house visiting my sister, the detectives that have been placed in our home to protect us from a deranged murderer have taken it upon themselves to arrest Lord Northmoor at the say so of an emotionally unstable and very amateur actress?"

"I believe that adequately sums up what has happened." Malton nodded.

"Actress?" The detective echoed.

"She most certainly is not a professional." Evelyn stepped closer to the detective. "But clearly she has used what *skills* she has to fool you. Whilst the Dowager Countess has threatened to report you to your superior officers, I am more than happy to actually do it. I would like you to get the Chief Constable on the telephone immediately. Please let him know that Lady Northmoor, the younger daughter of Sir Horace Hamilton, wishes to speak with him."

"Sir Horace Hamilton?" he repeated feebly. Evelyn almost felt sorry for him as he had turned quite green.

Her father had been a Member of Parliament until he retired shortly after the war. There wasn't a single person in a position of power in the county of North Yorkshire that did not know Sir Horace Hamilton.

Evelyn stalked to the telephone and held it out to him. "Why are you still standing there? Hurry it along."

It took long, agonising minutes for her to be connected to the Chief Constable in York. He did indeed remember her father and apologised profusely for the embarrassing error in judgement made by one of his junior officers in removing Lord Northmoor from his home. He promised to speak to Tommy personally as soon as he arrived and ensure he was brought back home forthwith.

Evelyn passed the telephone back to Detective Inspector Andrews and turned back to the butler. "Thank you, Malton."

"Lady Emily is waiting for you in the drawing room,"

They had taken barely two steps before, unsurprisingly, Emily appeared in the doorway. She had very clearly been listening to everything that had happened.

"A double gin and tonic is in order, I believe," Aunt Em said brightly.

Evelyn flopped onto a chair and looked imploringly at Malton, who had stationed himself next to the drinks tray. "I believe I am in need of a triple."

"As I said previously, absolutely magnificent." Emily nodded approvingly. "I shall join Lady Northmoor in a triple Malton. Thank you."

Chapter Fourteen

It was late evening before Tommy arrived back home. Evelyn greeted him at the door, though Malton had beaten her to it in order to open it for his new master.

She gave a most unladylike squeal of pure delight and launched herself into his arms. "I cannot even begin to tell you how much I've missed you!"

Not caring that Malton was standing right there, that the two uniformed officers standing sentry outside the front door were staring, and the detectives had come out of the old smoking room, Evelyn kissed her husband resoundingly on the lips.

"Gosh!" Tommy exclaimed. "I think I'll arrange to be arrested more often if this is how I'm greeted when I return home."

"You mustn't even joke about such things." Evelyn grimaced. "I had to break out the big guns to get you home."

"Oh dear," Tommy said, not sounding at all sorry. "You had to mention your father's name?"

"Indeed."

"Oh, my poor darling." Tommy laughed. "Do you need a gin to recover?"

"I believe Aunt Em and I rather emptied the gin bottle before they had even served luncheon."

"How scandalous! You must have missed me terribly." Tommy leaned forward and kissed Evelyn's forehead.

"Dreadfully," Evelyn agreed. "Now I fear we must rush to get ready for dinner, so I do not disgrace the family any more than I already have today."

Hand in hand, they headed toward the staircase. "You could never do that, darling."

As soon as Tommy had closed their bedroom door behind them, Evelyn burst into laughter. "Did you see the look on the detectives' faces when you came back through the door? They were nearly as furious as when I mentioned my father's name and made them call the Chief Constable."

"He was very apologetic," Tommy said. "Banged on about how it must be seen to the public that they are investigating the murders independently but that arresting and taking me out of the house was a step too far."

"I will have to deal with Lillian and her part in this after dinner."

"How exciting," Tommy said. "Can I watch?"

"She needs to know that things are now very different, and I will not stand for her awful behaviour, especially when it affects the people I love."

"I think the new you, the Lady Northmoor you, is rather thrilling." Tommy caught her around the waist and drew her closer to him. He kissed her thoroughly. "I believe, as Lord Northmoor, I can probably put dinner off until we're ready."

"And I believe," Evelyn said, slapping his hands away, "that we need to concentrate on proving who the murderer is and presenting that person to the police so you can live long enough to savour being Lord Northmoor. After all, the last person with that title barely managed to enjoy a full day."

"As I just told you," Tommy flopped back onto the bed with his hands folded behind his head, "I find the new in-charge and dominant you incredibly alluring. You are not helping me want to dress for dinner by being so…"

"Bossy?"

"Commanding," he retorted.

"Even when I am trying to tell you that if we don't find out who's killing off your relatives, you might very well be next?"

"Ah." He grimaced. "That does rather sober up a chap's romantic intentions."

"You haven't even asked what I found out this morning when I spoke with Milly."

"*I* have been a little busy being arrested and driven all over the county," Tommy grumbled.

"And *I* have been busy trying to clear your name," she replied tartly.

"There must be news. Tell me all about it." He grinned as she held up a hand and readied herself to tick off points.

"Isobel and Oliver met in less than ideal circumstances," she began and put up a finger. "Shortly thereafter, Oliver's wife died mysteriously."

"What happened to her?"

"Well—" Evelyn shrugged. "Milly did not know how she came to be in a coma or how she died quite so quickly after Isobel and Oliver began a relationship."

"Intriguing," Tommy commented.

"It is," Evelyn agreed. "But I don't know how that might relate to either Charles or Eddie. Unless they had information about Oliver's wife and her untimely death. I don't know that part yet."

"We will have to speak to both of them again."

"I think we need to talk to everyone again," Evelyn said. "We know more now than we did when we first spoke to them and now Eddie is dead too, we must work out if the two are linked."

"They must be, mustn't they?"

"The only person I know that directly benefits from both of them being dead is you, darling."

Tommy pulled a face. "Which is why they arrested me."

"Well, that and because Lillian told the police she was afraid of being in the same house as you after you threatened Eddie and he died."

"Did she?" Tommy shrugged. "That woman is an absolute menace."

"And although her lady's maid told Doris there was no way she could have recovered and gone outside to kill Eddie, she looked fine when she came downstairs when we all returned."

"I agree," Tommy said. "We cannot rule her out. She could have been faking how much the alcohol had affected her. For all we know, she could have been drinking water all afternoon and appearing intoxicated was a clever ruse. She is definitely not to be trusted."

"Unfortunately, given what has happened, I don't think we can trust anyone." Evelyn sat on the bed and put her hands in her lap. "I feel quite afraid."

Tommy knelt on the bed and crawled forward until he was behind her. He wrapped his arms around her, resting his chin on the top of her head, and holding her tightly against his chest.

They stayed in the embrace for long moments until Brown and Doris arrived to help them dress for dinner.

***

After dinner, Evelyn went through into the drawing room with the other ladies. Although she was tired and emotional after the events of the last few days, she did not want to put off the important conversation she needed to have with Lillian.

Neither did she want to talk to the other woman without witnesses. Not that she thought Lillian would agree to a private meeting with her either, she would be much too wary after the stunt she'd pulled having Tommy arrested.

Evelyn didn't waste any time in speaking directly to Lillian. "I understand you do not feel safe in the house with my husband present?"

"If you will insist on boring me," Lillian drawled. "Can you at least wait until I have a drink in my hand?"

"Of course," Evelyn said pleasantly. "Take your time."

She sat in the armchair nearest the fireplace, opposite Aunt Em, who sat in the matching chair. Evelyn believed that by speaking to Lillian calmly and allowing the other woman to think she was in control, it would give her the upper hand.

Lillian poured herself a drink, but did not offer anyone else one, and then sat on the arm of one of the sofas, a foot swinging back and forth, which revealed entirely too much leg for a grieving widow. "I think that murdering rogue should be in a prison cell, where he belongs."

"I see," Evelyn said.

"I don't know why they released him so soon. They should have thrown away the key."

"I dare say that would have pleased you immensely."

"And made me feel safe in my own home," Lillian retorted quickly. Her leg stopped swinging, the only sign that she had realised her slip up.

"We shall see about that in the morning," Evelyn said. "Tommy has asked Westley to produce Eddie's will, should he have one, so we can finalise all property matters tomorrow."

Lillian's eyes narrowed suspiciously. "What do you mean?"

"Based on how desperately unsafe you feel," Evelyn said. "And as I very much want to keep my husband home with me, I thought a suitable compromise would be for you to take one of the cottages located on the grounds."

"What?" Lillian howled. "You cannot do that!"

Evelyn curled her nails into her hand in an effort to hold on to her temper. "We are thinking only of you. You are, in fact, the one who raised the issue of your safety. The police have agreed to station an extra uniformed officer outside the door of whichever cottage you choose so you will have peace of mind."

"But…but what shall I do for meals? For…for…" Lillian finished her drink and banged the empty glass onto the table at the end of the sofa. "You will not get away with this!"

Lillian flounced from the room, her behaviour making Evelyn even more aware than she already was that she may well have just increased the anger of a murderer.

"Oh dear," Isobel said in her nervous little voice. "This is just dreadful. I simply cannot wait to get home."

"I am so sorry for your distress," Evelyn said. "You are quite correct. This has been an awful time. You must miss your children terribly."

Isobel nodded. "Do you think they will force us to stay here much longer?"

"I am afraid that is out of my hands. The police have repeated their request that everyone stay in the house until they apprehend the culprit or they conclude their investigations, whichever should come first."

"They don't seem to do an awful lot to bring that about," Julia grumbled.

"Well said," Isobel said, her voice muffled as she raised her handkerchief to her face.

"If it would help," Evelyn suggested. "Lord Northmoor and I could ask the police if I could bring your children and their nanny here whilst they complete matters?"

Isobel shuddered. "Absolutely not."

Evelyn's cheeks heated in embarrassment at the other woman's curt tone. "I'm sorry, I thought it may help."

"I love my children!" Isobel cried in a high, strangled voice. "I would not bring them into this…this…house of death."

Isobel left the room, though it had to be said that her exit was much less noisy and not full of the drama of Lillian's.

Evelyn very much wanted to follow their lead and run from the room to bury her head in her pillow and sob until she fell asleep.

All she had ever wanted was a quiet life after the chaos of her childhood. When Tommy returned from the war, she had believed she had everything she would ever want. Now her entire existence had been turned upside down. She was living in a house that she had no idea how to run, with staff she did not know how to manage and with her adored husband accused of murders she was certain he did not commit.

Chapter Fifteen

By morning, and fortified with a substantial breakfast, Evelyn was ready to bring this terrible situation to an end. Isobel, it seemed, was hovering over the line of insanity and Evelyn wasn't really surprised. The woman had been a highly strung sort before people had started getting killed in front of her face. Now her hands permanently shook, and her eyes had a wildness about them that was unnerving. Whilst Evelyn didn't have any children, she had Nancy, and she wasn't at all sure how she would cope should she not have the comfort of her dog and, of course, Tommy.

Sadly for Isobel, she did not seem to be blessed with the type of husband who put his arms around her in times of stress and allowed some of his strength to seep into and fortify her.

Evelyn had already asked Mrs Chapman to arrange for her staff to get one of the spare cottages ready for Lillian. Barring anything unexpected in Eddie's will, that particular thorn in Evelyn's side could be despatched to her new home that very morning.

On this occasion, only the family members and Dr Mainwaring were settled in the library for the reading of Eddie's will. Now the police were present in the home, Tommy had deemed it unnecessary to have anyone in the room other than family or those who were mentioned.

"Despite my urging following the passing of his father, Edward Christie did not update his will following Charles's death."

"Positively useless," Lillian snarled. "Could that man not do a single thing he promised?"

She had phrased it as a question, but since no one knew how to answer it, the room remained quiet. Evelyn found it amazing that, if Lillian and Westley were still involved in a passionate affair, the lawyer had not intimated to Lillian the terms of her husband's will.

"Of course, the will was drafted such that there are subsidiary clauses dealing with what should happen if one of the named beneficiaries should predecease the testator."

"Perhaps you should just get on it with," Lillian suggested, her features showing only displeasure with Westley and no trace of any affection whatsoever.

"Edward Christie's will mirrors Charles's exactly," Westley said, "in that he sets out the same clauses regarding primogeniture and the expectation that the estate should pass to the next in line after himself. He does not name that person, but of course we all know that to be Thomas Henry Christie. The clause reiterating forfeiture of the estate, should the person who inherits be found guilty of obtaining the estate by criminal means, is repeated."

Lillian stared at Tommy, pure loathing in her expression.

"There is just one personal bequest." Evelyn noted Lillian's look of pure satisfaction at Westley's words. "And that is to Dr Mainwaring. As a personal thank you for his work as the family physician, Eddie has left a bequest of five thousand pounds."

"No others?" Lillian hissed. "After everything I have done for him, that man has not left me so much as a penny nor a stick of furniture?"

Westley shook his head, his voice cool and measured. "I'm afraid not, Mrs Christie. I know that Mr Christie intended to update his will on the occasion of a child being born. But sadly, that was not to be."

Dr Mainwaring shifted in his seat and looked at Lillian oddly. Evelyn's breath caught in her throat. Did the doctor know something about Lillian they did not? Could it be possible that Lillian was indeed with child? Evelyn dismissed that idea immediately. If it were possible Lillian thought she could be pregnant with an heir who would oust Tommy, she would have said so. Though quite how that would be reconciled with the fact she had openly, and quite brazenly, admitted to several affairs Evelyn did not know.

If it were not Lillian's pregnancy that had caused Dr Mainwaring to look so uncomfortable, what else could be the reason? It would be incredibly difficult to find out, given the oath he had taken as a physician. Immediately her mind began working through possibilities of other ways she could find out what the doctor was hiding. Perhaps he was aware of her infidelities and the mention of a child had given him the exact same thought as Evelyn— though she didn't know how one went about proving a child was not legitimate when there was knowledge of affairs. As far as she was aware, there was a presumption that any child born to a married couple was legitimate.

"So, barring the authorities being able to prove that I have done something I know myself to be wholly innocent of, the estate including the house, grounds, land et cetera belong to me?" Tommy rose and moved to stand next to Westley.

"That is correct, My Lord."

Tommy gave a single nod. "Excellent. Well, in that case, I would like to engage you to update my own will immediately. In addition, perhaps we could complete plans for housing suitable for a Dowager Countess?"

"A…" Westley shot a bemused look at Lillian. "I don't understand."

"It's very simple," Tommy said smoothly. "Lillian has made it clear that she feels very uncomfortable being in the house with me, as she believes me to be responsible for the death of Eddie and possibly Charles. Therefore, Lady Northmoor and I have agreed to provide the Dowager Countess with a home within the grounds for the duration of her life."

"That is definitely in order," Westley recovered quickly. "And we can certainly formalise those arrangements into your will."

"We are prepared to provide the Dowager Countess with one member of our household staff on a temporary basis. We expect that she will wish to engage a staff of her own choosing. We will also provide the Dowager Countess with a yearly allowance so she may run her own household."

"Yes." Westley nodded vigorously now. "That is all very proper."

"What if I wish to remain living here?" Lillian's question was laced with menace.

Evelyn was about to answer but Tommy turned to face Lillian, with an expression on his face that suggested pure ice was running through his veins. "Unfortunately, that is not an option. We cannot guarantee your safety and we have plans for our new home that would be best achieved by you living in alternative accommodation that we shall subsidise."

"You cannot guarantee my safety!" Lillian now looked imploringly at Westley. "You see now how he threatens my wellbeing?"

Westley looked uncomfortable but gave Tommy a small smile. "I do not believe that is what Lord Northmoor meant at all."

Something clicked inside Evelyn's mind and she realised how swiftly and easily the solicitor had aligned himself with Tommy, to the detriment of Lillian. Could it be that Tommy would put lots of work his way and therefore be useful to him, whereas Lillian no longer had anything to offer him? Except that didn't quite make sense since what had Lillian previously offered Westley except for the very obvious? She had no power over Eddie and no interest or dealings in the estate whatsoever.

"So, I am to move out?" Lillian asked in a small voice.

For a moment, Evelyn almost felt sorry for the other woman until she reminded herself that Lillian was a devious piece of work and was probably playing yet another of her many parts. As Evelyn had noted to the police, Lillian was not a professional actress, but she was certainly very good at play-acting in order to get what she wanted.

Evelyn did not know why she was making the effort. Who in the room would have any sympathy for Lillian? They were all too well aware of her obnoxious personality. The only person who was looking slightly affected by the proceedings was Dr Mainwaring. He was definitely hiding something, and Evelyn made it top of her list of priorities to find out what it was.

***

The room cleared, leaving Tommy with Westley. The lawyer looked awkwardly at Tommy. Their most recent conversation had not been particularly amicable.

"Look," Westley said awkwardly. "About before...I wanted to apologise if I caused any offence."

Tommy thought the same now as he did then—the other man was not even slightly sorry about his affair with Lillian. He seemed bothered only that it had become common knowledge. It had been

Tommy's intention to use the pretext of drafting a new will to talk to Westley and find out what he could about the murders. He would then engage the services of a solicitor whose morals and ethics were more aligned with his own.

However, as it was not at all prudent to let his intentions become known at that time, he waved a dismissive hand towards Westley. "Think no more of it."

"I appreciate that, old man," Westley said. "Now, shall we sit down and get to business?"

The solicitor sat behind the desk, leaving Tommy to pull up a chair. The other man's presumption in choosing that particular seat for himself, in what was now Tommy's home raised the hairs on the back of Tommy's neck.

Would Westley have sat in that chair for a meeting with Charles? Tommy was certain he would not. He probably wouldn't have dared do so in a meeting with Eddie either.

In Tommy's mind, that showed an incredible lack of respect. If he had not already decided to find a new legal representative, that single act of discourtesy was decisive.

"I presume you will require a new will drafted along the same terms of that of Charles and Eddie's?"

Tommy nodded. "I do. I also wanted to ask about the term preventing someone who has committed a crime from benefitting. Is that not taken care of by the criminal law?"

Westley shrugged carelessly. "It did not matter how many times I explained that to Charles, he simply wanted it added into the written document."

"And you did that with a codicil rather than writing out a whole new will, even though his will was outdated?"

"Indeed, those were Charles's instructions." Westley nodded as though considering something of great importance. "It was my firm belief that, at that time, Charles believed Eddie might do something to hasten his departure from this earth so he could inherit."

"If that is true, there's no doubt Lillian most likely encouraged Eddie," Tommy mused out loud. "I remember when they were first married, they seemed very enamoured with each other. I was most surprised to learn recently that they were both involved in extra-marital relationships."

Actually, Tommy did not believe Lillian had been in love with Eddie when they married. She had most definitely been besotted with the money, the house, and the dream of one day becoming Lady Northmoor. Of that, there was no doubt.

"Of which Eddie was well aware," Westley commented. "That is one of the primary reasons why he chose not to alter his will when he became Lord Northmoor, despite my urging that he did."

"Why did you think he should?"

"Well, simply to keep matters tidy. No loose strings."

Tommy did not attempt to hide his confusion. "What loose strings? What was there to keep tidy? Eddie inherited everything completely from Charles, other than a few personal bequests. He was not likely to leave his sisters more money, given they had only just inherited from their father."

"It's customary for a new will to be made when there has been a death in the family."

Tommy spoke his mind. "Perhaps that is because the solicitor wishes to make himself some more money. Surely the time to make a new will is in the event of a marriage, or a child being born. Those are the occasions that a chap wishes to make certain those dearest to him will be taken care of properly."

"I take exception to your suggestion," Westley said, his demeanour belying his words, as he put the cap back on his pen and slowly and deliberately folded his hands and laid them on the table, "that I encouraged Eddie to make a will for my own financial gain. And, after all, it was you who suggested earlier that you wished to engage me to update your own will and legitimise any provisions you wish to make for Lillian."

"The Dowager Countess," Tommy snapped. Westley's over familiar manner and complete lack of courtesy were straining the last vestiges of his self-control. He wanted to ask if the other man intended to take up residence in Lillian's cottage with her, but he would not lower himself to the solicitor's base level.

Instead, Tommy stood and looked down at Westley with every bit of disdain he felt. "I believe this meeting is over."

Westley did not rise from the desk but began tidying the papers in front of him.

"Thank you," Tommy said with as much restraint as he could manage. "You may take your belongings with you. I will require use of my own library from now onwards."

"But…" Westley must have realised that he had hugely underestimated Tommy. "But I must have a room to work in."

"My understanding is that you have one," Tommy replied, and, at Westley's quizzical expression, he continued: "It is in your offices in the high street."

"But I cannot leave this house and I have work to do."

"I'm afraid, my good fellow," Tommy injected as much sarcasm as he could into those last three words. "That there isn't any work for you to do here in the house. Therefore, I do not see how you will require an entire room, or any other space, so I shall not be providing you with any. As regards leaving the house, you are quite at liberty to bring that issue up directly with the police."

"I have never been treated in such an underhanded manner!" Westley blustered.

"I believe that's what most of the young ladies have to say after they have unfortunately been in your company for any length of time," Tommy retorted sharply.

"You have just made a very grave error." Westley bundled his paperwork together and headed towards the door, stopping to point at Tommy from halfway across the room. "A very grave error indeed."

Tommy couldn't help feeling much as Evelyn had felt the night before after her confrontation with Lillian—what if one of them had just confronted the murderer and by doing so, put themselves in mortal danger?

Chapter Sixteen

Evelyn made her way outside to walk Nancy in the gardens approximately five minutes after she had seen Julia leave. Though the woman had told her when they had last spoken privately that she was not a very good shot, they had evidenced was evidenced the previous day on the moor. Evelyn could not allow the fact that she liked the other woman to affect her opinion regarding who the murderer could be.

Julia was down by the river again, this time standing on the bank. Evelyn could see no one in the distance, and there appeared to be no furtive kissing under trees this morning. Despite what Westley had told Tommy, insisting that he had no feelings for Lillian, the risks he had taken in pursuing his attraction for her made Evelyn think he was not telling the truth and there was much more to it than simply a passing interest.

"Good morning," Evelyn said brightly as she approached Julia.

Julia turned slightly, no welcoming smile on her face. "Morning."

"It's another beautiful day." Evelyn moved to stand next to Julia as Nancy took a flying leap from the grass to land in the middle of the stream.

"It would be better if our every move wasn't tracked." Julia looked back towards the house and nodded towards the figure of one of the uniformed police officers who watched them both from the side of the stone building.

Evelyn shrugged. "They are only doing their job. And, I must admit, they do make me feel a little safer."

Julia turned to look at her, genuine confusion on her face. "Why on earth do they make you feel more secure?"

"Just their presence in the house," Evelyn said.

"They were here when Eddie was killed, but it didn't stop that from happening." Julia pointed vaguely in the direction where Eddie was shot. "Right now, we could both be in danger and be dead by the time the police managed to run over the lawn to us."

Evelyn shivered despite the sun beating down on her. "I hadn't thought about it that way. I suppose I simply believed that the police being here would put the murderer off from striking again."

"That is possible," Julie said doubtfully. "But whoever shot Eddie took an enormous risk. Any of us could have turned around or seen the identity of the shooter, or they could have been a terrible shot and hit one of us instead. The murderer has a clear agenda that they were willing to follow despite the gamble they were taking."

"Speaking of gambles," Evelyn said softly, not keen to raise the subject, but knowing she needed to see Julia's reaction to her learning the secret regarding ownership of the school. "I did hear about the awful way your father lost control of the school."

"The old earl should never have held my father to a bet he made whilst much the worse for drink and being goaded by his cronies."

"Unfortunately, I do not believe that men care about a bet that was made whilst drunk or about the morals of accepting such a bet." Evelyn watched Nancy playing in the cool water and wished she could do the same. Unfortunately, even two days ago as plain Evelyn Christie, she wouldn't have dared take off her shoes and stockings and paddle in the stream. Today, as Lady Northmoor, she was aware more than ever of the very deep divide between what was, and was not, acceptable.

"Men and morality do not belong in the same sentence," Julia snapped. "I presume you are here to speak to me about the absolutely repulsive request that Charles made of me before he died."

"Are you referring to his suggestion that you admit a certain young student into your school?"

"It was not a suggestion, it was a demand! Despite the fact I have not been given access to adequate funds to properly manage my school," Julia said with an element of pride in her voice, "I have ensured that it is run correctly and to an exceedingly high standard in respect of educational attainment and moral soundness. I was then told that I must relax my strict entry guidelines."

"How very trying," Evelyn murmured, not wanting to say too much, so she did not stop the flow of Julia's words.

"Quite." Julia nodded. "If I allowed that particular pupil into my school, I would most definitely lose many others, parents who would not wish their child to associate with…"

"A child born out of wedlock."

"Yes," Julia agreed. "And still more parents would remove their children from the waiting list."

"But Charles, and Eddie, were prepared to cause the school to lose both its moral integrity and money simply to give this child an education?"

"Indeed." Julia reached down as Nancy dropped a stick at her feet and threw it for the dog to chase. "They suggested to me they wanted the child to grow up as a gentleman and so he must come to me for schooling rather than attend the village school."

"Do you think their plan was to somehow attempt to legitimise this child so he could eventually inherit?"

Julia shrugged. "That I do not know. However, as we have already said this morning, men and morality do not go well together. I know of no legal way that child could have become Eddie's legitimate heir."

"And you told Charles and Eddie that you refused to add this child to your school roll?"

"Actually," Julia said. "I did not. I am aware that persuading me to do just that was behind the invitation to secure my attendance at the manor this weekend. However, I did not speak to either of them in a private capacity before Charles died."

"But, I presume, and especially after you received that request, that you would do anything in your power to get the school back under the control of your family?"

Julia turned and looked at Evelyn for long moments before she eventually spoke. "Yes, I would. It is more than simply an educational establishment to both myself and my father. We have both put our hearts and souls into the place, especially my father. And I would do absolutely anything so it is owned by the Davenports again. My father deserves to have the one single mistake he made in his life be reversed before he dies."

"Your father is ill?"

"No." Julia's eyes sparked as she spoke. "He is not, I am simply trying to make it clear how desperately I want the school returned to us."

Evelyn's attention was caught by Nancy, who had returned to the stream, and was nudging something with her nose. The sun reflected from the item and Evelyn moved forward to see what it was.

"What is it?" Julia asked as Evelyn leaned carefully over from the bank of the stream to retrieve the item.

"Nancy has found a decanter."

The find rather put paid to the questions Evelyn still wanted to ask, but she needed to take the evidence straight into the house to the police.

Her mind worked through what she had learned as she hurried towards the house. Just how desperate was Julia? Desperate enough to kill?

Clearly Julia was very close to her father and would do anything to make him happy. Whilst Evelyn didn't have that depth of emotional connection with either of her parents, she had it for Tommy and she knew that as devoted as Julia was towards her father, Evelyn was towards her husband.

And there wasn't a single thing she would not do for him.

***

Each of their guests had developed their own way of coping with being restricted to the house and grounds. Whilst Julia liked to walk outside, and could sometimes be found reading in the library, Oliver could almost always be found in the billiard room. Tommy had never yet seen the portly man attempt to play the game. However, he could usually be found sitting in one of the maroon leather chairs with a tumbler of amber liquid at his elbow and a cigar hanging from fleshy lips.

He was absolutely ruining Tommy's rather naïve view of a vicar who spent afternoons writing Sunday sermons with a bible and nothing stronger than a cup of tea to fortify him through his work.

"Do you mind if I join you?" Tommy asked.

"In a drink or simply in the room?" Oliver looked up and Tommy did his best not to allow the shock he felt from showing in his face.

The other man's eyes were bloodshot, and it looked much like he hadn't stopped crying since last time they had spoken. Oliver was a broken man.

"I say," Tommy said gently. "You don't look at all well. Should I get Dr Mainwaring and see if there is anything he can do for you?"

"There's nothing he, nor anyone else, can do," Oliver said morosely. "As I told you previously, Isobel is to have a child that does not belong to me."

"What will you do?"

"What can I do?" Oliver spread his hands wide in a gesture of complete defeat. "The deed has been done."

"You won't leave Isobel or turn her out of your house?"

"Of course not." Oliver shook his head decisively, as though that hadn't even been a consideration. Yet how could the other man not have explored that option if his wife had indeed been unfaithful? "We're married."

"And that's for life?"

"Yes," Oliver nodded firmly. "Yes, it most certainly is."

"Because you're a man of the cloth?"

"Not just that." Oliver took a sip of his neat brandy. "But I believe in the sanctity of marriage regardless of my religious leanings."

Tommy wondered when this belief of Oliver's had begun, because if what they had found out so far was correct, he certainly hadn't practiced what he preached when he had met Isobel. He took a deep breath. He would not get to the bottom of things if he did not ask the hard questions. "Did you feel that way when you were married to your first wife?"

Oliver did not display any shock that Tommy was aware he had been married previously, nor were there any signs that suggested he felt guilty. In fact, it dismayed Tommy to notice, there was no emotion on his face at all. "Yes."

"But you went on to have a relationship with Isobel whilst your wife was still alive?"

Oliver put down his glass and turned sad eyes onto Tommy. "Have you ever known anyone in a coma?"

Tommy shook his head. "I have not."

"Then you cannot possibly understand," Oliver said, with no censure in his words. "Hilary was alive, but not alive. She lay in a hospital bed for months, breathing, but not living. You cannot begin to understand how utterly devastating that was."

"And meeting Isobel comforted you?"

"Not in the way you are insinuating." Oliver exhaled. "At the beginning, being with Isobel reminded me of the early days with Hilary. Instead of feeling sad when I looked at Hilary, I could remember when she was young and full of joy and happiness. Just as Isobel was at that time."

"And that helped?"

"I could tell myself that Hilary would not have wanted me to sit by her bedside and stop living in the same way as she had stopped living."

Personally, if it were him, Tommy would absolutely want Evelyn to sit at his bedside holding his hand and praying for him to wake. He would not want his wife to take up with some bright young thing that reminded her of happier times and allowed some sort of weird logic to convince her that it would be what he wanted.

"And now? Do you still think Hilary would have wanted you to find someone else?" Tommy was honest enough to admit that he would want Evelyn to mourn him until the day she died. Of course, he adored her, he wanted her to be happy—but with someone else? He just couldn't stomach that.

Oliver barked a short, mirthless laugh. "Of course not. She would have been horrified that she was laying there, and I was allowing myself to be led away from what I believed and knew to be correct and moral by a young woman whose only advantage over Hilary was that she could give me the affection that I craved."

"And now you feel horribly guilty?" Tommy guessed.

"Now I hate Isobel almost as much as I hate myself," Oliver said morosely.

Tommy thought for a moment, allowing what Oliver had said to settle in his mind before he spoke. "Since you discovered her infidelity?"

"No," Oliver said. "I felt guilty even as I stood in the church putting a ring on Isobel's finger not two months after Hilary's death."

"And your shame has grown as the years passed?"

"Absolutely." Oliver nodded vigorously in agreement. "As each year passed, and we had a new baby, so I remembered Hilary and how she had become ill when pregnant with our first child. We lost that child and at the same time, I lost the Hilary I knew and loved. She never recovered from the efforts of trying to give our child life. Now each time Isobel gives me a healthy child, and fully recovers, I become more and more resentful of her."

Tommy felt horribly ill-equipped to deal with such an outpouring of raw emotion. He was not a father, and he could not imagine being in the position Oliver had found himself in, but even so he did not believe he would have behaved in the same way. Yet there was something so undeniably sad about Oliver that Tommy couldn't help but feel a deep compassion for the other man and his suffering.

"And, if I have understood you correctly, you married Isobel because she was pregnant with your child and this fact has compounded your misery?"

"That is correct," Oliver said heavily, as though a great weight were bearing down on him. "And whilst I have this burden that I live with and, I will tell you, it feels as though it's strangling me little by little as each day passes, my wife is now bearing another man's child. It's a tragic sort of irony really, isn't it?"

"I think this is one of the most desperately sad stories I have ever heard," Tommy said honestly.

"So you see," Oliver said, finishing his drink in one large greedy gulp. "I drink to forget. I wake up with no end to my self-recriminations, and then I see Isobel who is the very embodiment of the most shameful time of my life."

A sudden movement in the doorway caught Tommy's attention, and he looked around in time to see Isobel fleeing into the corridor.

"Oh dear," Oliver said apathetically. "I fear she heard every word."

Chapter Seventeen

Evelyn tapped on the door of the room that Isobel and Oliver had been sharing during their stay at Hessleham Hall.

"Go away!" The muffled response was barely audible through the thick wood door.

"Isobel, it's me, Evelyn. Please let me in, I'm very worried about you."

Long moments passed before Evelyn heard a shuffling behind the door, and it eventually opened. Isobel held a creased handkerchief up to her face.

"Get it over with!" Isobel said in a high, strangled voice. "Your husband will have told you the whole sordid tale."

Actually, Evelyn believed there was still a very important part of Oliver, Hilary and Isobel's story that she did not yet know. However, she had not come upstairs to harangue the distressed woman. She genuinely only wished to offer sympathy.

"I have absolutely no intention of passing judgement on anything that you may or may not have done," Evelyn said gently. "As I said, I'm concerned about you."

Isobel stifled a sob but did not look convinced. "Why would you care about me?"

"I care about anyone in great torment and I wholeheartedly believe that you are suffering an immense amount of pain. I could not, in good conscience, know that was going on in my own home and not at least attempt to do something about it."

"You can't make me feel any better." Isobel shook her head emphatically.

"Perhaps not," Evelyn acknowledged. "But I can certainly sit with you and ensure you don't feel any worse than you already do. May I come in?"

"Tommy told you, I'm sure, that Oliver knows about the baby?" Isobel hid her face as she opened the door wider to let Evelyn into her room. "I'm so ashamed."

"It's not an ideal situation," Evelyn said frankly. "But it must be worth you sitting down together and talking honestly to see if you can both find a way forward?"

"I can't see how." Isobel began to cry again. "I heard what he said. He told Tommy that he cannot stand to look at me because I remind him of a time when he was ashamed of his own actions. Our children remind him of the one he lost with Hilary and how that pregnancy caused her illness and eventually her death. And if that wasn't all bad enough, I am now certain I am expecting another man's baby."

"Maybe…" Evelyn began. This was so difficult. She did not feel sufficiently experienced to have this sort of conversation with any woman, let alone one she did not know very well. She was realising just how sheltered her life had been until this moment, as people experiencing things that were completely foreign to her surrounded her. "Maybe that makes you both even?"

"Even?" Isobel wiped at her face. "In what way?"

"If Oliver feels so horribly guilty because of his relationship with you, now you have essentially done the same as him, you have both sinned."

Isobel shook her head. "But don't you see? He doesn't hold himself responsible for sinning against Hilary. He holds *me* responsible for that, as though I made him do it. That is the belief that has festered inside him all these years and brought him to the point he is at now where he cannot bear to even look at me."

"Does his faith not help him at all?"

Isobel sniffed. "Not at all. It's all very new to him really."

"His faith is new?" Evelyn repeated, feeling hopelessly confused.

"Oliver became a vicar after we married, just before we moved to Hessleham."

"What did he do before then?" Evelyn asked. This information certainly went a long way to explaining why Oliver didn't act at all like she had expected a vicar would.

"His father had a shop, he helped out there."

"And Hilary?"

"Her family were not impressed with the marriage. They felt that she had not made a very good match. They had money, and he was a shop owner's son."

"So you moved away after you got married, and Oliver became a vicar, but he hasn't been able to move on from his guilt." Evelyn put her head on one side, trying to work through the situation in her own mind. "But that doesn't explain what happened with you."

"Why I started seeing another man, do you mean?"

Evelyn nodded. "Of course, if it's too difficult, we can talk about something else."

"It's very simple." Isobel shrugged. "I didn't know about the depth of Oliver's feelings until today. But I knew he didn't feel the same about me as he had. As I told you the other day, my life has been all about raising babies since we married. I was truly lonely."

"So you began seeing this man because you were looking for affection that Oliver was not giving you?"

"In part," Isobel said. "But also, because he needed me. I believed he had genuine feelings for me, but he was using me for his own gains."

"Does he know about the baby?"

Isobel looked horrified at the suggestion. "No, he doesn't. And I will not tell him. He must never know."

"Is he married?"

"No." Isobel shuddered and the look of pure fear that crossed her face made Evelyn feel very uneasy. "But he is a very evil man."

"What shall you do?"

"I do not know," Isobel sobbed. "I simply do not know how our marriage can survive what has happened, yet what other alternative do I have?"

Evelyn had no more words of comfort to give and knew that they would be empty platitudes. What could she possibly say to make the poor woman feel better about the decisions she and her husband had made some years ago?

She stayed with her, stroking the other woman's hair until, quite exhausted, Isobel fell asleep.

***

Tommy caught up with Dr Mainwaring at the stables. Until Malton reminded Tommy that the estate offered a stabling service to those in the village without enough land of their own, he had quite forgotten that was yet another function that the estate performed.

Neither had he known that Dr Mainwaring was a horse owner. Actually, when he considered it, he realised that he knew very little about the village doctor—a man to whom his cousin Eddie had left a monetary bequest that seemed to make very little sense.

"Good afternoon," Tommy greeted the other man. "I'm just catching up with things around the estate. I had no idea you stabled horses with us."

"Two." Dr Mainwaring nodded. "I trust you are not planning any changes to arrangements such as mine."

"Absolutely not," Tommy confirmed. "I see no reason why I would wish to change things that my uncle and cousin have agreed to."

"Jolly good," Dr Mainwaring said, reaching out to rub the nose of the grey horse in the box in front of him. "It's very convenient to be able to come up to the estate and ride whenever I have the spare time."

"I don't suppose you know how many other people have similar agreements?"

"I'm afraid not but the chap in charge of the stables is very helpful. I'm sure he will know."

"Of course," Tommy nodded. "I shall ask him."

It concerned Tommy greatly that he had no idea how many people visited the estate on a weekly basis and how many of those visits were necessary. Perhaps it was simply the untimely deaths of Charles and Eddie that left him feeling that his newly gained property was far from safe and secure. He didn't want to put up gates, but neither did he want to worry about Evelyn's welfare constantly while he was out and about on the estate.

"Was there anything else?" Dr Mainwaring asked, a suspicious look on his face.

"I had been meaning to ask you what medicine my uncle was taking before he died. I heard some talk that a bottle was missing."

"His prescriptions had no relevance to his death. Your uncle was murdered."

"I am aware, but I would still appreciate you answering the question. There is no reason not to, as I believe your oath regarding patient confidentiality would not apply following his death."

"That is correct though I see no reason you would need this information."

"Is there a reason you are refusing to give it to me?"

"None other than my professional integrity." Dr Mainwaring turned away from his horse to look at Tommy. "I suppose the police have the information and could easily pass it on to you."

"Absolutely," Tommy agreed.

"He was on tablets to keep his blood pressure under control."

"What would the effects on Charles have been should someone have removed his medicine for any substantial length of time?"

"Very little over a couple of days. He was on a low dose, given more as a preventative measure than something he absolutely needed to take in order to stay healthy."

"You cannot think of any reason for it to have been removed?"

"No. As I said to the police, I believe this to be information that does not progress their investigation at all."

"The bottle contained tablets, not medicine?"

"That is correct."

"Could the tablets have been coated with poison and then the bottle replaced with a new one so there would be no traces of hemlock found on the medicine bottle?"

"Possibly but I do not believe that is what happened. The police asked if I could confirm that the bottle was the original I had given to Charles and I was, and am, certain that it was."

It certainly seemed that this was a complete red herring, yet Tommy was reluctant to let it go. Why would someone go to the trouble of removing Charles's medicine bottle, only to return it, for no reason at all?

"You seemed very surprised to find that Eddie had left you some money?"

"It was such a long time ago that I didn't expect him to recall his promise."

"The will was made some years ago," Tommy reminded him. Though, that was not the important part of either the bequest or what Dr Mainwaring had said. "Why did he promise to leave you money?"

"I helped him." The doctor shuffled his feet and looked toward the house, as though he wanted someone to come out and rescue him from Tommy's questions or run there to avoid their conversation.

"In what way?"

The other man stared at Tommy before seeming to decide about something. He shrugged. "I don't suppose it matters anymore now he's dead. Though I would ask you to be discrete, for Lillian's sake."

"Does it have to do with Eddie's extra-marital affairs?" Tommy enquired. "Because, if so, I must tell you they will not cause Lillian any upset. I know that she is completely aware of them."

"Yes, there was a child." Dr Mainwaring confirmed. "I helped Eddie, and the lady concerned, to find a family for the baby. The couple who took the child could not have their own children. Eddie said he wanted to reward me for my help and for my discretion, despite my protestations I had done it to try to secure a happy future for the infant."

"I understand there is also another child in the village who is said to be Eddie's son."

"That particular young lady refused, quite adamantly, to give her child up. I know because Eddie tried to come to a similar understanding."

Tommy couldn't help but wonder how many other children Eddie had sired in the village. Whilst he understood families who could not have their own children would welcome a baby into their home, and probably not put much thought into how that baby came about, it made Tommy very uneasy about his cousin's behaviour.

"How very strange that Eddie seems to have a number of illegitimate children, yet none with his wife." Tommy looked toward the roof of the stable. It wasn't at all comfortable for him to talk about matters such as this—even with a doctor.

Dr Mainwaring pulled out a handkerchief and wiped his brow. "Indeed."

"Do you know anything about that?" Tommy pressed.

"I cannot…"

"You know something but cannot tell me because of the Hippocratic oath?" Tommy interrupted, knowing immediately that his guess was correct.

The doctor looked increasingly hot and bothered, even though the spot where they were standing between the stables was very shady.

"I cannot share what I know." Dr Mainwaring looked away. "Please don't ask me anything else."

Tommy could not stop now, not when he felt that he was close to finding out information that might prove crucial in finding out who had murdered Charles and Eddie. "Are you able to tell me something that helps in a way that does not break your oath?"

The doctor looked directly at Tommy now. "There are doctors in London who specialise in helping women to not have babies, or to plan their pregnancies so they do not have more than they would like or can afford."

Tommy immediately understood the meaning behind the doctor's words. "Or have none whatsoever!"

The other man looked as though a weight had been lifted off him, now this particular secret was out. "Indeed."

Chapter Eighteen

After he'd spoken to Dr Mainwaring, Tommy headed out into the warm mid-afternoon sun to find Jack Partridge.

"How goes things?" Tommy asked.

"It's been a difficult few days." Jack held out his hands, palms up. "I just don't know what is going to happen next."

"Yes, it's been eventful, to say the very least."

"I have given a lot of thought to our discussion."

It wasn't really the other man's contemplation Tommy had been hoping for; it was a change in his work ethic. He wanted Jack to take decisive action to eradicate poaching on the estate but firstly to stop the arrangement he had with the local butcher. "And what conclusions have you come to?"

"Geoffrey Beckett is excellent at catching rabbits."

"I'm sure," Tommy said, trying to remain calm but feeling angry at the blatant thievery that was going on at the estate's expense. "But that is not a skill I will praise when he is doing it on my land. Without permission."

"Oh no, sir," Jack said. "I mean…My Lord…I'm so sorry. It takes some getting used to, calling three different gentlemen 'my Lord' on three separate days."

Tommy smiled reassuringly. "I understand. Please continue."

"What I meant to say regarding Geoffrey is that perhaps there would be scope to have him continue to catch rabbits but on behalf of the estate rather than against it, as it were."

"And still sell them to the village butcher?"

"Yes, it's a very large estate, as you are aware. It would make sense that we allow a skilled hunter to take excess wildlife from the grounds in exchange for a monetary profit."

"And how could I be expected to trust you both?" Tommy asked. "After all, it seems that for some time, the both of you have been stealing from the old earl. How could I be sure that I would receive the correct profit of the game you sold on to the butcher?"

"If I may, My Lord?"

"Speak freely," Tommy said.

"The old earl wouldn't even listen to my idea, as I have just outlined it to you. I tried to speak to Mr Eddie, but he said he didn't have the time to learn nor care about such matters."

"So, you and Geoffrey did it anyway, and lined your own pockets in the process?"

"That is true." Jack flushed. "But I also have a solution regarding that, if you would like to hear it?"

Tommy nodded. "Go on."

Jack produced a small notebook and pencil from one of his pockets. "I have kept a careful record here of all game sold to the butcher. If we may come to some agreement, My Lord, as to what we would charge the butcher, perhaps we can then make an arrangement for Geoffrey and I to pay back what we have taken without permission?"

Tommy liked the estate manager's idea to recompense the estate, but even more he appreciated Jack's knowledge of the estate and how that would help him increase profitability. "I think that is certainly something we can discuss so we can reach a mutually beneficial outcome."

"Thank you, My Lord. I appreciate your compassion."

"You must not take it for soft-heartedness," Tommy said sternly. "I can see that if we work together, it will benefit the estate. I am therefore willing to overlook what you have done in the past so we can forge a beneficial partnership from now on."

"I understand that." Jack nodded contritely.

"And if you have any other ideas at all that would benefit the estate, please come to me." Tommy looked off across the moors to the spot where Eddie had been shot. "I mean to be fully involved in as much as I possibly can."

"Of course, My Lord." Jack followed Tommy's gaze. "Have the police said anything more about Eddie's death?"

"Not a word." Tommy adjusted the brim of his hat in an attempt to shield his eyes from the sun. "As far as they, and I, am aware, no one who was out on the moor that day saw anything at all. Let alone anything unusual."

"I still cannot fathom that someone would dare to do something so very brazen."

"You're right." Tommy nodded. "It was as incredibly audacious as it was dastardly."

"And whoever it was is an excellent shot." Jack went on. "If they had stood and actually aimed the shotgun at Eddie, someone would have been sure to see. But whoever it was must have just swung their gun and fired."

Jack made some excellent points. Tommy had considered them himself but listening to someone else say what they thought out loud caused him to reassess what could have happened. "Do you think, therefore, that there is a chance that whoever shot Eddie perhaps meant to shoot someone else and Eddie was a mistake?"

"On the contrary," Jack said. "I think whoever killed Eddie is a quite remarkable shot and not only are they cold-blooded but also incredibly dangerous."

Tommy considered his words, which he agreed with, but there was one other scenario he wanted to get Jack's opinion on. "Could the shot have come from somewhere else, do you think?"

"The police asked me that." Jack looked over at the house, as though imagining someone leaving the building and making their way over to the moor, without being seen, to then shoot Eddie. "But no, I don't think so. For a start, the gunshots were all in the area where we were. One coming from a different part of the estate would have been immediately obvious. We were all firing at the grouse and it wasn't until someone turned around and saw Eddie on the ground that any of us realised he had been hit."

"Who first noticed the accident?" Tommy unconsciously repeated the words they had told the police when they returned to the house. Of course, it had not been an accident, yet he still found using the word 'murder' in relation to both his uncle and his cousin so incredibly surreal.

"The vicar's wife." Jack grimaced. "She screamed loudly and for a very long time."

Jack was right. Isobel had seemed particularly affected when she first saw Eddie dead on the moor, though she had quickly assumed an air of total indifference. Was that significant or was it of more relevance that Julia, who had claimed to be a poor shot, had quite easily shot more grouse than anyone else that afternoon and hadn't seem at all upset at the sight of a dead body?

Tommy hoped he wasn't being desperately naïve, but he didn't believe the murders had anything to do with Jack. He put out his hand for the other man to shake. "Let's hope we can put this nasty business behind us very soon and get on with working together for the good of the estate."

"I very much hope so, My Lord."

***

Later that evening, Tommy and Evelyn were talking about the recent developments in their room before getting ready for dinner when a tremendous shout reverberated along the corridor. Tommy rushed to the door and opened it, looking to his left where the guest rooms were situated.

"What is it?" Evelyn asked from behind him.

Oliver Turnbull came hurrying from his room. "Please! Someone help my wife!"

Tommy and Evelyn left their room and ran down the corridor to where Oliver stood looking incredibly agitated. He hovered outside, as though he didn't want to go back in, but knew he should.

Tommy went straight to the bed where Isobel lay prone and fully dressed on top of the bedspread. Evelyn put a hand on Oliver's shoulder and helped him into a chair in the corner of the room. "What happened?"

"I found her this way," Oliver's voice broke as he spoke. "I tried to wake her up, but she won't. It's like Hilary all over again. I just can't bear it."

Oliver put his head into his hands and sobbed. Evelyn murmured what she hoped were reassuring words as Tommy gently shook Isobel's shoulder and said loudly and firmly. "Mrs Turnbull? Isobel? Wake up!"

After receiving no response, Tommy looked over at Evelyn with a grimace. "I'll go for Dr Mainwaring."

"Is there a pulse?" Evelyn wondered.

"I don't feel confident enough in my abilities to even attempt to find one. I shall fetch the expert."

Tommy hurried from the room, and Evelyn patted Oliver ineffectually on the back. "When did you last speak to Isobel?"

"I tried earlier," Oliver managed through his tears. "But she refused to talk to me after she heard me speaking with Tommy…that is…his

Lordship...and she came up here believing that I hated her."

"But you don't?" Evelyn moved away from Oliver, a thought coming to her. "Does your wife take anything to help her sleep at night?"

"I don't hate her, not really." He lifted a shoulder in utter resignation. "I think it's easier to blame another, rather than admit to the part you've played in a particularly unhappy situation."

Evelyn pulled open the drawer in the small table next to Isobel's side of the bed. "Does Isobel have any powders?"

Oliver blinked, then slowly blinked again, as though he was coming around after being knocked out. "Yes, she takes something to help her sleep."

"And does Dr Mainwaring prescribe those powders?"

"Yes, yes, that's right. The village doctor."

Evelyn found the box easily in the drawer and opened it to see how many sachets were left. Two. That wasn't particularly odd if the prescription was an old one. However, it may go some way to explaining Isobel's current state if she had taken more than the prescribed dose.

Tommy returned quickly with Dr Mainwaring, who was half dressed for dinner, and half in his day clothes—it made for a very strange sight given the doctor was always so well turned out.

"These powders were in the nightstand's drawer." Evelyn thrust them into the doctor's hands as soon as he came into the room. "There are two left."

"Two?" Dr Mainwaring almost shouted the number, clearly exasperated. "That is quite wrong. Christie, telephone for an ambulance immediately!"

"What can I do?" Evelyn asked as Tommy ran from the room.

"She needs immediate hospitalisation to have her stomach pumped," the doctor said urgently.

"Until then? There must be something we can do whilst we wait for the ambulance to come."

"There's something we can try, but I don't know how much success we will have."

"Then we must try," Evelyn said decidedly. "Oliver, will you help us?"

"I shall pray," Oliver said in a voice that suggested he had already given up all hope.

"We must get Mrs Turnbull to her feet," Dr Mainwaring said, reaching across Isobel's prostrate form and manoeuvring her to the edge of the bed. "If we can try to walk whilst supporting her, the movement and being upright may cause her to regain consciousness. Ideally we would hope that she vomits and expels the drugs she has ingested."

He shook his head. Evelyn did not know whether it was because he was going to try something that he did not believe in or because he was afraid of the damage that would already have been caused to Isobel's body by the excess sleeping draught.

The doctor levered Isobel up to a sitting position, Evelyn put one of Isobel's arms over her own shoulders whilst Dr Mainwaring did the same on the other side. With significant effort, Evelyn got to her feet and between her and the doctor they began half dragging, half carrying the unconscious woman along the rug at the side of the bed.

Tommy came back into the room and immediately took over, casting a disgusted look at Oliver who sat staring at nothing in particular whilst his petite wife struggled with the much taller Isobel.

The prayers Oliver stated he would offer for his wife must still be inside his head because there was no evidence of him offering any vocally.

"Is there anything I can help with, My Lady?" Mrs Chapman asked from the doorway, a concerned look on her face.

"What more may we do, doctor?" Evelyn asked. "Should we get fresh water for Mrs Turnbull to drink should she regain consciousness?"

"Yes, water. And hot, sweet tea. And a receptacle should we manage to wake Mrs Turnbull up."

Evelyn turned to Mrs Chapman, who responded immediately. "I shall bring those items right away, My Lady."

"Do you see any changes to her face?" Dr Mainwaring panted in exertion as he and Tommy turned and began walking back towards Oliver. "It's very difficult for me to see from here."

"She looks as though she might have slightly more colour," Evelyn said uncertainly. "Though it's very difficult to tell whether that is real, or I am seeing it because I desperately want her to recover."

"You have nothing to feel guilty about," Tommy said sharply. "It was I who was speaking in an indiscrete way with Oliver that allowed us to be overheard."

Evelyn shrugged doubtfully. "I could have done more. When she fell asleep, I left her all alone. I should have guessed she would do something like this. She said she feared her marriage was over and she was left with no alternative."

"Talk to her!" Tommy barked at Oliver. "Talk to your wife and tell her you have made a terrible mistake in what you said and the way you have dealt with your relationship. Tell your wife what she needs to hear and perhaps she will wake up."

Shock at Tommy's tone, together with total reluctance, played across Oliver's face as he perched himself on the end of the bed and began talking to Isobel.

"Dearest," he said, voice cracking with emotion. "I have not treated you in a way that would allow you to realise the very deep regard that I have for you. During our marriage you have selflessly borne and raised our children with no help or gratitude from me."

Evelyn blinked away tears. What a shame such heartfelt words could not be heard by the person who desperately needed to hear them.

"I understand," Oliver went on, nodding to himself. "I understand completely why you felt that you had no escape from your pain other than to take too much of your sleeping draught. All those years ago I told you that the only way we could be together was if Hilary was no longer alive. And when she died soon afterwards, I allowed myself to believe it was God's will. Over the years, I came to believe it was because of something that you had administered. You knew how to do such things because of your job in the hospital dispensary. And the guilt I felt for putting that sequence of events into motion and then over the years endorsing what you had done by remaining silent led me to experience a guilt from which I could not escape."

Evelyn stared at Oliver, horror invading every pore in her body at his uncensored words.

"So, I treated you with less and less regard until, starved of attention and affection, you ultimately sought those things from another man. And here we are, my darling. You are unconscious. Just as Hilary was, the circle is now complete."

Oliver again dropped his head into his hands and wailed in earnest. That awful sound was suddenly punctuated by Isobel coughing and gagging. Evelyn rushed forward with the chamber pot she had retrieved from underneath the bed.

The vicar believed his wife to be guilty of causing his first wife's demise. Clearly, what they had also learned from Oliver's ramblings was that Isobel also had the knowledge to have brought about the death of Charles, though Evelyn couldn't imagine what possible motive Isobel would have for killing Charles. Or, for that matter, Eddie.

Unless the two men had found out her terrible secret and then threatened to reveal it? That would surely be enough for Isobel to feel that she had no choice but to silence them both.

Chapter Nineteen

After the ambulance arrived to take a semi-conscious Isobel to the hospital, Tommy and Evelyn had spoken to the police to explain that they were confident they knew who the murderer was and had asked that they be allowed to present their findings in the drawing room after dinner.

Whilst initially very reluctant, especially as Tommy was still a suspect, they had eventually agreed when Evelyn had pointed out that it would be the detectives who would make the arrests and that accomplishment would surely go some way to mollify their Chief Constable.

Detective Inspector Andrews had written off what they were attempting to achieve as simply 'parlour games' but he had ensured that all guests were present in the drawing room for what he termed their little charade.

Tommy began by looking at each of the individuals sitting in the drawing room—Aunt Em, who was sitting slightly forward with a flush on her cheeks, Lillian who was sat by herself with a thoroughly bored look on her face.

Westley looked as imperious as ever, his ankles crossed neatly and both hands folded around a tumbler that looked as though it contained rather a large measure of brandy. One thing was for certain: when all the guests could finally go back home, the alcohol consumption in the house would drastically reduce.

Tommy had sent word that he wished both Jack Partridge and Geoffrey Beckett to be present, as Jack had been in the house when Charles was killed. They sat together on one of the sofas, looking very uncomfortable and horribly out of place.

Dr Mainwaring leaned against the fireplace, nervously adjusting the cuffs of his suit jacket. Julia Davenport sat with her hands primly folded in her lap, having refused a drink. Although, to outward appearances, she looked as though she were taking this very public unveiling of the murderer in her stride, Tommy noticed her swallowing compulsively in a classic show of anxiety.

Oliver sat in one chair to the side of the fireplace, having refused all efforts to get him to go to the hospital with his wife. For once, he did not hold a tumbler containing alcohol. Although his eyes were dry, he had that look of a person surviving on the very edge of their emotions.

"I shall start by speaking to each suspect in turn and then going through our conclusions as we find them. Aunt Em," Tommy said, looking at his great aunt. "I shall start with you."

"That is absolutely proper." Aunt Em smiled.

Tommy inclined his head and returned his great aunt's smile. "Whilst the death of Uncle Charles's wife, Florence understandably devastated you, I do not believe that you avenged her passing by killing Charles—however much you did not like him. I do not propose to make any further comments on the death of my Aunt Florence. I cannot possibly hope to reach any accurate conclusions regarding her death."

"I'm not sure how you think you can come to any deductions at all." Lillian got up from the seat opposite Oliver's and went over to the drinks tray to make herself yet another gin and tonic. Tommy was quite amazed she could function so normally when she rarely finished a meal and everything she drank was alcoholic. "You're not even with the police anymore."

"No," Tommy agreed smoothly. "But as you can see, the police are here in the room, and they have given me their permission to speak to everyone. Now, may I continue?"

Lillian had her back to Tommy as she finished making her drink. She did not say more, and so he took her silence as a cue to continue.

"You were also inside the house when Eddie was shot and therefore could not have shot him. Neither have we been able to determine a motive for you to kill Eddie."

"Apart from him being particularly odious and my very least favourite great nephew?" Aunt Em enquired imperiously.

"Those things aside." Tommy inclined his head. "We can rule you out of being a suspect. To conclude: whilst you may have had a motive for killing Charles, we do not believe that you had the necessary knowledge to bring about his death."

"We should make it clear at this point," Evelyn intervened. "That we do believe the same person to be guilty of killing both Charles and Eddie."

"Thank you, darling." Tommy smiled fondly at his wife. Once this was all over, they could get back to life as an ordinary married couple. Of course, ordinary might be a stretch as things would be very much different at the manor to the life they had led in their comfortable little cottage, but he was hopeful they could find a new normal here at Hessleham Hall.

"As Evelyn stated, we feel that the same person killed both victims. Therefore, it follows we do not believe Eddie killed his father. Although there were reasons for us to suspect him at the beginning, we don't now believe that original assumption is correct. We do think it was Eddie who took his father's blood pressure medication and then returned it to Charles' room following his death.

Whether he did that in an attempt to bring about an illness in his father, we cannot possibly know for certain, but we can speculate that perhaps that was his intention. Dr Mainwaring has assured me that a few days without medication would not have caused an illness in Charles serious enough to kill him and, of course, we are aware that his death was brought about by hemlock poisoning. None of our investigations have led us to believe Eddie would have had knowledge of or any pharmaceutical experience."

Tommy paused then to gather his thoughts. "Our last point in relation to Eddie is the fact he was seen holding the brandy decanter after we took his father upstairs ill. Malton has confirmed that the decanter in use on Thursday evening prior to Charles becoming ill was not the same one he used after dinner. Therefore we believe that Eddie was looking at the decanter and quite probably realising it was not the usual one. We will come back to what we believe happened to the original one later."

Evelyn moved slightly forward from where she stood at Tommy's side. "I will now continue and discuss our findings in relation to Lillian Christie."

Lillian clapped her hands together in mock delight. "Oh, how very exciting! I can barely contain my glee."

"I have also been waiting eagerly for this moment," Evelyn retorted. "Though I'm sure for very different reasons than yours."

Lillian gave Evelyn a look that was close to admiration before her expression changed to a very unbecoming sneer.

"Regarding the death of Charles, you had both the motive and the opportunity to doctor the brandy. Whether you have the knowledge to do such a thing, we cannot be sure. However, our investigations have led us to believe that you have friendships with various different *gentlemen* who could possibly give you access to such information.

Your reaction when Charles' will was read showed us you were expecting a bequest, which would certainly have given you a motive to want him dead."

Lillian shrugged, looking as though she couldn't be less interested in the discussions. "I cannot argue with any of that."

"With regards to the death of your husband, you were again upset not to have received an individual bequest from him. Whilst your lady's maid did say you were incapacitated when Eddie was shot, we didn't feel that we could rule out you were faking intoxication and did in fact come outside and shoot him. However, Tommy and I were both there, as were other witnesses who all agreed with our firm belief that the shot did not come from the direction of the house but from the moor. Indeed, no staff members reported hearing anything out of the ordinary in relation to the sounds of the shots."

"Good golly," Lillian said, sarcasm lacing her words. "So, you conclude the killer is not me?"

"Very reluctantly," Evelyn agreed. "Though I must say, your conduct is not at all what one would expect from a lady."

Lillian gave Evelyn a thunderous look and rose from her chair as if intending to leave the room.

Detective Inspector Andrews held up a hand. "I'm afraid no one is to leave the drawing room until we say so."

"Well, at least this evening's little performance is more entertaining than the ordinary, very dull conversation I have to endure," Lillian said dramatically. "Now who is next for my very favourite and incredibly *amateur* detectives?"

***

Tommy took over, turning to his two outside staff next. "Thank you very much, both of you, for coming up to the house this evening."

"You said it was important, My Lord, so it is our pleasure to assist in any way we can." Jack spoke whilst Geoffrey bobbed his head in agreement, twisting his cap between nervous fingers.

"You were obviously here for dinner on the evening Charles was killed," Tommy began. "However, we do not think you are familiar enough with the layout of the house to have brought about Charles' death. As you were outside as part of the shooting party when Eddie died, it is possible that you shot him. We are aware, as has already been discussed with you, that there was some talk that you and Geoffrey here could have been involved in a poaching scheme and that perhaps you would wish Charles and then Eddie dead so your scheme did not come to light."

"There's no *could have* about it!" Lillian's voice was harsh as she stared venomously at Tommy. "I know they have an *arrangement* because I caught them in the act."

"And you certainly made me pay to ensure your silence," Jack hissed as he turned in his seat to look directly at Lillian.

"I made you pay?" Lillian screeched, enunciating each word carefully and at top volume. "How very dare you!"

"I apologise," Jack said, only the slightly amused smile playing on his lips showing that he did not mean his words. "I do understand how incredibly unseemly it is to have a discussion about how you blackmailed me into making love to you. Especially in front of all of these people."

"You! You...absolute reprobate!" Lillian hurled her empty glass in Jack's direction.

With all the deftness of a man accustomed to working outside with the unexpected, Jack caught the missile before it had a chance to do any damage—either to himself or to the floor behind him.

"This goes beyond unseemly," Westley said, uncrossing his ankles and bracing his hands on the sides of his chair. "It's a downright disgrace. Partridge, apologise to the Dowager Countess immediately, otherwise I'm afraid I will have to ask you to step outside to resolve your terrible slur on the lady's character."

"You want me to step outside?" Jack hissed. "For telling the truth? I think we are both aware that she is no lady."

"The truth?" Westley pushed himself to his feet, fury etched on his handsome features. "As if a lady would ever entertain the likes of you!"

"Entertain? Let me tell you..." Jack also got to his feet.

Tommy moved to stand next to Jack and, with a reassuring hand on his shoulder, encouraged him to sit back down. "I don't think your relationship with Lillian is relevant, old man. Let's move on."

Westley, however, clearly did not want to move on. He stared across the room at Lillian. "You had an affair," he nodded his head in Jack's direction, "with him?"

Lillian raised her chin. "What of it?"

"But..." Westley appeared stunned as he sank back down onto his chair, all the fight gone out of him. "I cannot believe what I am hearing."

"So, as I was saying," Tommy continued. "I don't believe that Jack had the means to kill Charles, although he certainly had a motive. I would not embarrass either party regarding the illicit affair, but now that it is out in the open, it's clear he also had a motive for murdering Eddie if we were to take the view that Jack wanted Eddie out of the way so he could be with Lillian. We do not believe, however, that this was an affair involving love—on either side."

"So, you are simply writing him off?" Westley said. "Lillian is right. You are absolute *rank amateurs*."

Evelyn watched as Westley shook his head in anger and then made a concerted effort to get himself back under control. The only way women could possibly fall for him was because of his exceedingly good looks and possibly an abundance of fake charm, because he really was not a pleasant man at all.

"Moving on now to our next person of interest, who is Julia. Again, it is hard to see how Julia would have had a good enough knowledge of my uncle's habits in order to kill him. However, her father had been a regular visitor here until he had a falling out with Charles. We do believe it is possible, therefore, that he could have passed along useful information to his daughter. In addition, as a teacher, we cannot dismiss the possibility that Julia would have either a grasp of poisons and how they can be utilised or the ability and intellect to research the subject. Despite telling me she did not shoot regularly and so was not an excellent shot, I found the opposite to be true when we were out on Saturday afternoon. We believe that Julia therefore had the means, the opportunity and the motive to kill first Charles and then Eddie."

"Gosh…well…" Julia stuttered. "I wish I could argue with your logic and convince you of my innocence, but I don't have a single thing to say in my defence. I don't have an alibi for either murder and, as you have so rightly pointed out, I have two excellent reasons to wish both Charles and Eddie dead."

"I never thought I would hear myself say this," Aunt Em said. "But Lillian is quite correct. This is jolly decent entertainment."

"Aunt Em," Tommy chided. "It is not supposed to be amusing. We are attempting to uncover a murderer."

"Oh, I know." She waved a hand flippantly in the air. "But nothing exciting ever happens, and this is the most fun I've had since Eddie fell down the stairs when he was showing off trying to slide down the bannister."

Tommy and Evelyn looked at each other and smiled. They really would have to work very hard in the future to keep Aunt Em entertained on an evening in a way that didn't involve murder, deceit and grown men threatening each other. Achieving such a feat would be an incredibly tall order.

Chapter Twenty

"Perhaps we should continue," Tommy suggested. "There's still quite a lot of ground to cover."

"Whose secrets are we to hear about next?" Aunt Em asked with a devilish glint in her eyes.

"I am to discuss Dr Mainwaring next." Tommy raised his eyebrows in reproach at his aunt and then turned to the doctor. "We know little about you, Theodore. In fact, out of everyone present we know least about you."

Dr Mainwaring looked steadfastly back at Tommy without blinking. "I am an open book, My Lord. What you see is absolutely what you get."

"There was the minor matter of a monetary bequest," Lillian said snidely.

"That was a personal matter between me and your husband," the doctor explained.

"You may as well share it." Lillian swept out an arm, encompassing everyone present. "Everyone has a secret. We may as well know the nature of Eddie's that meant it gave you money. Clearly it was something he wished to remain private."

"That is correct." Dr Mainwaring nodded. "And so, it should stay confidential. As, I am sure, you would wish your remaining personal business to stay your own."

"Not at all," Lillian said brightly. "What is the point in me keeping things to myself now? Who have I left to disappoint?"

"Certainly not yourself, dear," Aunt Em said, with entirely too much glee.

"At least I have allowed myself to have genuine enjoyment in my life." Lillian flung her words at Aunt Em with every bit as much power as she had used to throw her glass at Jack. "What have you done except live your entire life as a spinster in this house?"

"I would rather live, and then die, knowing I had one genuine love than an entire village full of lovers." Aunt Em steadfastly met Lillian's nasty glare.

"One true love?" Lillian scoffed. "And what did he do? Escape when he found out what a disgusting old trout you are?"

"Actually no," Aunt Em replied calmly. "We met in India but before he could come back to England so we could be married, he was caught up and killed in the Bengal army mutiny in 1858. I was a girl of nineteen then and by the time I felt able to contemplate a new suitor the world had moved on without me and the young men had all married other girls."

"Oh, Aunt Em," Evelyn whispered. "How desperately sad."

"It was rather," Aunt Em agreed. "Now, Lillian, do please cheer me up by telling me more of your sordid antics."

"I believe we were at the part where Dr Mainwaring was attempting to spare my blushes by not revealing something he knows about Eddie. Now that we have established I have no blushes that require sparing, perhaps you'll carry on, doctor?"

"If you insist. It was a gentleman's agreement, so I am breaking no vow of confidentiality by divulging the reason behind the bequest I received. As we are all no doubt aware, Eddie was not in the habit of remaining faithful to his wife and frequently took himself into the village…"

Tommy cleared his throat. "Maybe the ladies need not hear all the details."

"Of course...of course. My sincere regrets, ladies, if I went too far and offended your sensibilities."

It wasn't really likely, given the discussions they had already had that evening, but Tommy nodded his thanks for the earnest apology.

"There was a child," the doctor stated blandly. "Born to a village girl and Eddie asked my advice. I was able to find a family who could not have a child of their own and made arrangements for the baby to be taken to them. For my help, and also my discretion, Eddie promised to give me some money. I had quite forgotten about his undertaking until the reading of his will."

"Jolly strange of him to leave it in his will," Evelyn mused. "Given he cannot have expected to have died at this early age."

"Perhaps he thought it was amusing?" Dr Mainwaring suggested. "He could tell me honestly that had done exactly what he promised, he didn't actually specify that it would—or would not—be in his lifetime."

"That sounds like Eddie," Lillian agreed. "Always promising what he did not have."

Tommy thought it was probably best they move things along. Speculating on what Eddie had, or hadn't meant by leaving the doctor money in his will hardly mattered anymore. "And that's all we have for the doctor. He did not know about the bequest and so, although he had the means and the opportunity to kill both Charles and Eddie, we could not determine a motive for him to kill either."

"And so, we must now move on to the Turnbulls." Evelyn smiled sadly in Oliver's direction, but he either didn't see her show of sympathy or completely ignored it. "Again, a lot of the information we have gleaned seems to either make little sense or, at the very least, is contradictory."

"Only people with a guilty conscience try to top themselves," Lillian stated, then as accusing eyes were cast her way. "I don't know why you're all looking at me like that, it's true. Why would anyone kill themselves over Charles and Eddie dying unless they were guilty?"

"Perhaps she was just desperately sad," Julia suggested.

"I completely agree," Evelyn said, "with both of you. I think there's an element of both of those emotions behind Isobel's actions. Though, of course, we will not know exactly what she was thinking until she wakes up."

"*If* she wakes up," Lillian muttered, no doubt believing that she had spoken in tones so hushed that she would not have been heard. Unfortunately, excess alcohol never made a person quieter than they meant to be.

"We found out that Isobel had worked in the hospital both before, and then again during, the war. She worked in the dispensary so would have been well aware of how hemlock worked and could be administered. It's very difficult to find any motive that Isobel may have had for killing Charles and even less for Eddie, though we do think Isobel had means and opportunity for both, and Oliver certainly had the opportunity for both. What is less certain is whether Isobel would have been able to add the poison to Charles' drink without being detected, as she was not a usual visitor to the house."

"The poison was added to his drink?" Aunt Em asked sharply.

"That is what our investigations have led us to believe." Evelyn looked over to Tommy, "We must now conclude our findings."

***

"And so we move on to Westley, a man who has visited the house frequently and has been in the confidences of both Charles and Eddie. Whilst

Westley had the means and opportunity to kill both men, we struggled a little on motive until he was seen kissing Lillian with a passion that went beyond mere friendship. The fact that Lillian hotly denied an affair with Westley, despite being more than happy to admit to other affairs, made us think she was denying it to throw us off the scent. Then there was her reaction to not receiving money from either Charles or Eddie in their wills. It was hard to know if this was an act, because we do believe that Lillian is quite an accomplished actress, or a visceral reaction."

Tommy paused and watched Lillian as she preened at his praise of her acting skills. They had formulated a wild guess as to why Lillian wanted money in her own name, and this was their chance to put this theory to the test.

"How much were you expecting to receive, Lillian? How much were you promised?"

"You believe that they promised me a sum?" She looked doubtfully over at Tommy.

"We certainly do, and we think you were not just promised by Charles and Eddie, but by Westley too."

"Now, see here!" Westley called out, looking quite agitated. "You didn't call into question Mainwaring's professional integrity, so why are you insinuating I have broken the privilege between myself and my clients?"

"Dr Mainwaring didn't give me any reason to doubt his outstanding character," Tommy said smoothly.

"Is this charade nearly over?" Westley made a show of looking at his fingernails, but his expression of indifference was a little delayed as he had already shown how angry he was at the proceedings.

"It would be concluded an awful lot quicker if we didn't have interruptions every two sentences." Tommy spread his hands out in front of him in a gesture of hopelessness. "How much, Lillian?"

"Ten thousand pounds," she said, a greedy glint in her eyes.

"And if Evelyn and I were to gift you that money, the money that they promised you, would we be right in thinking you would go to America?"

"Of course she wouldn't!" Westley exclaimed, a quite desperate note in his voice. "Why would she go to America?"

"Because, of course, you believed that the plan was for her to marry you, after a brief period of mourning?"

"Your suggestions are quite ludicrous." Westley re-crossed his ankles. "And, actually, rather insulting."

"Lillian?"

"You and Evelyn would really give me all that money?"

They had been correct! Tommy paused and took in a deep breath to calm his nerves. He needed to play this perfectly for the plan to work. Now was not the time to celebrate the accuracy of their assumption, but to carry on being cool and calm to bring everything to a conclusion.

"I have a cheque prepared. I shall write in the amount." Tommy pulled the folded cheque out of his inside pocket, together with his pen.

Lillian looked a little crestfallen, as though she wished she had told him a much higher sum of money. Truth be told, Tommy would probably have paid her more money to get her out of their lives and as far away from their home as possible.

He leaned on a side table, completed the cheque, and crossed the room to put it into Lillian's hands. Her doleful expression immediately altered into one of pure joy.

"I must pack immediately!"

"Your belongings are being packed as we speak," Tommy told her. "For your move into one of the estate cottages. However, if you have now decided to leave Hessleham, you can move whenever and wherever you please, subject to permission from the police, of course."

"You are leaving? Just like that? After everything..." Westley's voice had lost all of its arrogance, and he now sounded like a man who was completely lost.

Lillian held on to the cheque tightly, and looked away from Westley, a small and very smug smile on her lips.

Before Tommy could even react, Westley was on his feet and propelling himself across the room towards Lillian. The solicitor had his hands wrapped around Lillian's throat before Tommy had even moved. Absolute chaos reigned for long seconds before the police and Tommy could prise Westley off Lillian and back into the chair by the fireplace.

"Cuff him!" Tommy demanded. Detective Andrews nodded at the uniformed officer guarding the library door to do as Tommy had asked.

Evelyn moved to see if Lillian wanted any help, but the other woman waved her off.

"I don't want your sympathy," Lillian said, a little unsteadily. "We are not friends, so let us not spend our last moments together pretending. As for you, Westley, you were nothing but a diversion. A plaything. Someone to dally with whilst I was waiting for my money and my ticket out of this absolute backwater."

Westley shook his head, total disbelief on his face. "But you said we would be together. We had a plan."

"I don't know what you mean." Lillian touched a hand to her throat, as though amazed she was still in one piece—or maybe it was just another one of her games and she was doing it for sympathy in front of the police. Who knew with that despicable woman?

"Our plan!" Westley screeched the words, his bound hands lifting from his lap as though he was trying to make a gesture but forgetting the police had placed him in handcuffs.

Lillian's eyes flashed in triumph. "Like I said, I don't know what you mean. I think you may be a touch deranged. Perhaps you need to speak to Dr Mainwaring about a little something for your nerves."

Tommy could see the moment Westley gave up. Sorrow and confusion left his eyes and a malevolence that Lillian would've been proud of entered his expression.

"Our plan, dearest," Westley's voice dripped sarcasm. "The one where Charles and Eddie were out of the way, Tommy was in prison for their murder, and you then discovered you were pregnant with Eddie's child."

"Let me stop you right there!" Dr Mainwaring held up a hand. "I cannot let this go on any longer. Mrs Christie has engaged the services of a doctor in London, at my recommendation, who supplies her with certain items to prevent pregnancy."

"But my child…our child…" Westley faltered.

She was more despicable than Tommy had given her credit for. He looked at her with open disdain. "Did you tell Westley you were pregnant with his child, intending to pass that baby off as Eddie's so you and Westley could control the estate on behalf of that child?"

Lillian looked sulky, but not at all repentant. "That was Westley's plan. He liked the idea of being lord of the manor, if not because of the actual title, then because of the role he would fulfil."

Suddenly, Tommy couldn't bear to look at her anymore. He turned to the police officers. "Get that creature out of my drawing room. And whilst you're at it, take her plaything with you."

Evelyn moved closer and placed a calming hand on his forearm. She leaned her head against his shoulder as Westley and Lillian were taken from the room.

Chapter Twenty-One

"What will happen to us?" Oliver lifted his head once the police had led away Lillian and Westley.

"That's not for us to decide," Evelyn said, moving over to sit next to Aunt Em on the sofa and opposite Oliver. "If you believe Isobel had something to do with Hilary's death, that's for you to resolve. Tommy and I have spoken about it and we don't feel that it's something that we should get involved with."

"But you will need to report Isobel for poisoning Charles, won't you?"

"How long have you suspected Isobel may have had something to do with Charles' death?"

"It all seemed to fit." Oliver raised red-rimmed eyes. "Of course, I knew she worked in the dispensary when we met. And although she had no reason to kill Charles herself, it's possible someone else had manipulated her to either tell them how to do it or provide them with the means to do it."

"Unfortunately, that's also the conclusion we came to. We think you are correct that another person coerced Isobel."

Oliver looked around the room, embarrassment clear on his face. "You're being kind by trying not to embarrass me and reveal everything in front of your guests but let me be frank. Not only did I say I believed Isobel was involved with someone else, but that she had become pregnant as a result. I suppose that must mean Westley will get that child he wanted after all."

"But why would she do that?" Aunt Em asked. "Why would she risk her family to get involved in a cold-blooded murder?"

"We've asked ourselves that," Evelyn said. "And our theory is that Westley either had knowledge of the circumstances surrounding Hilary's death, or perhaps he worked out that five children and a live-in nanny would be difficult to sustain on a vicar's wage. Perhaps Westley was asked to draw up a will for Oliver or Isobel and realised then they had money over and above what one would expect for a vicar."

"Where did the money come from?" Aunt Em asked.

"We mentioned Oliver's first wife, Hilary. The money was from her family."

Oliver looked hopeful for the first time in days. "Do you think Westley might have blackmailed Isobel into providing him with the poison? And she didn't cavort with him through choice?"

"Until Isobel wakes, or Westley talks to the police, we will not know that for sure. And, of course, either or both of them could lie. The only certainty we have is that Westley administered the poison into Charles' brandy and then replaced the decanter. It's our belief that the contaminated decanter was thrown in the river shortly before he was seen with Lillian by Julia. The discarded item was found by Nancy and passed by me to the police. However, due to it being in the water for a time, they could not get any usable fingerprints from it."

"So it also implicates Lillian?" Julia asked.

"Again, I fear the truth of that will never be known. She may have conspired with Westley, or she may have gone along with his plan having no active participation herself. We think the police will have difficulty proving anything against Lillian. However, we believe she will be more than happy to provide them with a full statement against Westley to get her own freedom."

"I understand what happened to Charles, but how did Westley kill Eddie?" Aunt Em wondered.

"Once more, the police will struggle to make a case against Westley for Eddie's death as there were no witnesses. However, the case against him for Charles' murder, particularly if Isobel and Lillian give evidence against him, is very strong. We believe he will hang for that crime and the police will probably not pursue the case against him for Eddie's death."

Oliver got slowly to his feet. "I should get to the hospital. I would like to be there with Isobel. Maybe if I had behaved differently, not allowed my own guilt for our relationship and for Hilary's death to rest completely on Isobel's shoulders, none of this would have happened. She is my wife, and I must stand by her, and not fail her as I failed Hilary."

"And the child?"

Evelyn could only imagine the terrible pain Oliver had gone through when he had lost his unborn child and his wife had succumbed to a coma. She admired the strength of the girl in the village who had allowed a childless couple to give her baby the life she could not. And now she could not help but think about the baby Isobel was carrying and what would come of it.

"We shall have to discuss that when the police decide what charges they will bring against Isobel."

Tommy moved to the door. "I shall ask Malton to have the car brought around. Our driver will take you to the hospital."

"As regards the child—" Evelyn found that she simply couldn't let the image she had conjured up in her mind go. "Should you have a need for help with that child, could you please let us know?"

"Why would you want to do such a thing?" Oliver shook his head in disbelief.

Tommy draped an arm around her shoulder and pulled her close. "My wife is correct. We would be honoured to assist, so please do contact us if you have any need."

"Is there anything you two will not bring to this house?" Aunt Em asked as soon as Oliver had left. "We've had murder, infidelity…"

"I must stop you there, Aunt Em," Tommy interrupted. "We have not brought the murder or the infidelity."

"Allow me to finish," Em responded grandly. "Murder, infidelity, possible blackmail and now I'm certain I just heard you offer to help with a child conceived on the wrong side of the blanket."

"In all fairness," Evelyn answered with a smile on her lips. "You were only saying earlier how you haven't been this entertained in years."

"Oh, I wasn't complaining, my dears, I was simply hoping you might warn me in advance. Whilst I may enjoy the new life I feel you will bring to this old house, I am most concerned my nerves might not be able to take the strain."

"I don't believe there is anything we can do that will shock you, Aunt." Tommy chuckled. "I would think it unlikely that anything we do would give you a moment's consternation."

"Are you quite finished for this evening?"

"Not quite." Tommy turned to Julia. "As soon as I can engage the services of a new solicitor, we shall have the school transferred into your name or, if you would prefer, that of your father. If you let me know, I shall make the proper arrangements."

"Why would you do that?" Julia asked in wonder.

"Because," Tommy said simply. "It is the right thing to do."

"I believe this rather wraps things up, My Lord?" Detective Inspector Andrews said as he moved forward to shake Tommy's hand. "I was very unsure about your scheme, but I have to admit that it worked rather well."

"The results exceeded our expectations," Tommy said modestly. "We had hoped that either Westley or Lillian would incriminate themselves, but for Lillian to turn on him completely should ensure his conviction."

"Absolutely." The detective agreed. "All that now remains is for us to remove the two of them from your home and allow you to get on with your lives peacefully."

"You are aware," Tommy said with a devilish glint in his eyes. "That I am to live here with these two ladies? I think peaceful is entirely unattainable."

Chapter Twenty-Two

"There is still so much I do not understand," Aunt Em said as Malton served the family with drinks.

"Such as?" Tommy asked.

"You say Westley Harrison shot Eddie?"

"That's right."

"Did I not hear over dinner last night what an absolutely terrible shot he was?" Aunt Em's forehead puckered in confusion.

"You did," Evelyn said as she nodded. "We believe he told us he did not like shooting and shot badly deliberately so we would not suspect him."

"What about the situation with the wills?" Aunt Em pressed. "I still do not understand why Eddie, and then Lillian, were so perturbed by the contents of what were very straightforward documents."

"We do have a theory," Tommy said.

"Then let us hear it!" Aunt Em raised her eyebrows in mock disgust. "What is the point in telling us you think you have it all worked out and then not sharing it with us?"

"Lillian clearly expected money," Tommy began. "We think it had been her intention to go to America and become an actress for some time and perhaps Eddie believed that would be a good idea. She was becoming less discrete with her affairs, and that would have been very embarrassing for him. We learned that Eddie had tried to secure a place at Miss Davenport's school for a child born out of wedlock to a girl from the village. Apparently both Charles, and Eddie, were keen that this child be raised a gentleman."

"We did not see the relevance of this information at first." Evelyn took up the story. "But as you suggested, Aunt Em, the importance of some of what we learned was not clear until we put together other pieces of the puzzle. We think Charles and Eddie intended to pay Lillian to pretend this child in the village was hers and concoct some story about her rejecting him as a baby."

"Then the child would be reunited with his parents here in the house following a period of schooling with Miss Davenport?" Aunt Em guessed.

"That is what we think," Tommy confirmed. "Shortly thereafter, Lillian would leave for America. Eddie would have his heir and Lillian would have her money."

Evelyn shuddered. "This has all been about greed."

"And children," Tommy added. "So many children have been affected because of the actions of their parents."

"You're thinking specifically of the vicar's children?"

Tommy nodded. "That is why we offered to help Oliver and Isobel if we could."

Aunt Em took a ladylike sip of her drink. "I see that now."

"They are the innocent victims," Evelyn said sadly. "Children should not have to live in the shadow of the sins of their parents."

Em nodded in agreement, and then a sly smile played on her lips. "It has been a long time since this house has had children living in it."

"And it shall be a long time before there are children living in it again!" Evelyn retorted.

"Oh Evelyn, dear," Aunt Em said. "I know you do not mean that. Simply listening to you this evening has shown me what a kind and compassionate person you are."

"We shall have children when the time is right." Tommy held up a hand as it appeared Aunt Em would say more. "There will be no talk about duty. Our children will be born because we want them and we are ready to be parents to them."

Even Aunt Em could not argue with that.

***

The following morning, Evelyn went downstairs to the kitchen. "Good morning!"

"My Lady!" Mrs O'Connell pushed her ample frame from the chair she was relaxing in.

"I was wondering if there is any dough for me to knead this morning?"

"We have no more gossip for you now that the investigation is over," Nora said, looking very put out.

"As I said to you when I was down here previously, whatever day that was." Evelyn waved a hand. "I mean for you to be my friends. I would be a terrible friend to only come and see you when I wanted something, wouldn't I?"

"But Mrs Christie—" the cook began. "Ma'am. That is…My Lady. You cannot come down here anymore."

"I can't?" Evelyn raised a querying eyebrow.

"A lady of your station cannot be in the kitchen with the likes of us."

"Well, what are we to do?" Evelyn mused, holding up her left hand. "I have remembered to leave my rings on my dressing table and so I am completely ready to get up to my elbows in flour."

Mrs O'Connell shared a baffled look with Nora. The young girl found her voice first. "If we are truly to be friends, My Lady, I think it is only right and proper that we give you some dough to knead, if that is what you wish to do."

"I completely agree." Evelyn nodded. "Mrs O'Connell?"

"Yes." The cook nodded. The expression of total confusion still had not left her face. "Of course."

"You need not look so afraid," Evelyn told her. "Who is to tell us we cannot do the things that make us happy?"

"But there has to be order," Mrs O'Connell said feebly.

"And so there shall be," Evelyn agreed. "Mrs Chapman would not allow me to run a disorganised house. I know that everyone here has a role to fulfil and I would not for a moment wish to disrupt that state of affairs. My mother is not a very conventional woman and although I decided many years ago I did not want to be at all like her, I think I have discovered that being unique has its advantages."

"Unique, My Lady?" Mrs O'Connell questioned. "I do not follow?"

"It is a very polite way to say my mother has always done what she has wanted, when she wanted." Evelyn laughed. "And I think I rather like that philosophy. Though I will, of course, take into account the orderly running of the house."

"Do all them words mean you will just come down to the kitchen when you want to bake something but not so's you will get in our way and stop us from working?" Nora suggested.

"That is absolutely correct." Evelyn smiled at Nora. "Now, Mrs O'Connell, do we have a deal?"

"Yes, My Lady." The cook answered, shaking her head in bewilderment. "I shall fetch the dough."

***

"We must at least have a conversation about it." Tommy looked up at Evelyn from where his head lay in her lap.

Evelyn absently smoothed back his blonde hair from his forehead whilst she collected her thoughts. "I am not against having children. I think I might even like them."

"That is a start," Tommy said.

"I honestly regretted not seeing Milly's children when I visited her about Isobel and Oliver."

"And you were desperately sad about Isobel's baby."

Evelyn closed her eyes as she remembered how sick she had felt when Dr Mainwaring gave them the news that Isobel would make a full recovery but that she had lost her baby. "That poor woman will never forgive herself."

"That *poor woman* taught Westley all he needed to know so he could kill Charles."

"I know that's true, darling, but I feel so very sad for her. What do you think will happen to her?"

"That is now in the hands of the judiciary system," Tommy said. "She has made a full confession to the police and is also the mother of five children. Those two facts may mean she is treated leniently. However, she is still an accomplice to murder."

"So she may hang alongside Westley?"

"Sadly, yes."

"Meanwhile, Lillian, who I do not doubt started all of this, is on her way to begin a new life in America. It does not seem fair."

"It absolutely is not," Tommy agreed. "But, as we feared, there is not even a bit of evidence against Lillian other than Westley insisting it was all her idea. He poisoned Charles, and he shot Eddie."

Evelyn sighed. "Let us talk about something else, I want to forget all about murder and dead bodies!"

"At the start of this, you were so excited to start sleuthing."

"And I have now decided all of that is not for me. I would like to enjoy a quiet life without people falling down dead all around me."

"A quiet life in the country sounds ideal."

"Doesn't it?" Evelyn leaned forward and kissed Tommy. "An absolute dream."

"You don't think you will get bored with too much quiet?"

"Absolutely not." Evelyn shook her head. "I have Nancy and you and this house to run, as well as all the other things I have to do as Lady Northmoor."

"No babies for us then just yet?" Tommy couldn't keep the disappointment from his voice.

"I don't think I am ready. Just look how I've been through this investigation—I've neglected Nancy."

"Darling, Nancy is a dog. We are talking about a human baby."

"But that's my point. If I allowed myself to forget about Nancy, who is like a child to me, then I will certainly be remiss about the needs of a baby when my mind is busy elsewhere."

"There's nothing wrong with having help with a baby whilst you are doing other things."

"My mother had help but look at what an absolute mess she made of parenting Millicent and I." Evelyn shook her head decisively. "My mind is quite made up. I don't want to be the same kind of mother."

"But you won't be, don't you see?"

"Obviously not," she responded tartly.

"The very fact that you are worried about if you'll be any good tells me you most definitely will be good." Tommy held up a hand to stop her protestations. "Now, at the risk of making you cross, do you think your mother has ever spent a day of her life wondering whether she's a good mother?"

"Oh, I have absolutely no doubt that she has not."

"And there we have it."

"Have what?"

"Proof."

"How, exactly?"

"Your mother was not concerned about her children at all, but you are worrying about whether you will be a dutiful mother to yours before they are even here."

"I think I may see what you are saying."

"Well, I hope you do." Tommy kissed the tip of her nose. "And I hope you can also see that accepting help with our child, when you choose that it is time for us to have one, is something that I absolutely insist upon."

"Our child will not be living on the top floor for us to visit once a day!"

"No, darling, it most certainly will not," Tommy agreed, amazed at his wife's quick change of mood. "Our child will be loved, adored and pampered. But he or she will also have time with the nanny so you can enjoy your dogs, your investigations and me."

"Do you know something?" Evelyn enquired.

"What would that be?"

"You really are the most perfect man."

"At last." Tommy grinned. "Something on which we agree."

***

Murder at the Village Fete, Book 2 in the Tommy & Evelyn Christie Mystery series is now out! Click the button below to add it to your kindle if you want to find out how the local Member of Parliament ends up dead in the stream at Hessleham Hall!

Get it here!

Murder at the Village Fete

Downton Abbey crossed with Murder, She Wrote...set in a Yorkshire village!

Evelyn Christie, the new Lady Northmoor, is looking forward to hosting the local village fete on the grounds of Hessleham Hall.

However, the last thing she expects to see on the morning of the fete is the local Member of Parliament face down in the stream at the edge of the lawn! Evelyn and her husband, Tommy, are once again called into action to find the dastardly murderer before he strikes again!

If you enjoy the glamour of bygone eras like 1920s Downton Abbey and gently, cozy mysteries set in the English countryside then you will love this new series.

Get it here!

A Note from Catherine Coles

Thank you very much for reading Murder at the Manor! I had so much fun writing this story and I very much hope you enjoyed reading it. If you did, please consider leaving a review. Not only do reviews help other readers decide if Murder at the Manor is something they might like to read but they also help me know what readers did, and did not enjoy, about my book.

If you would like to be amongst the first to know about my new releases, please join my monthly newsletter.

Click to join my newsletter

I have also formed a Facebook group for fans of cozy mysteries. It's a place where we can chat about the books we've read, the things we like about cozies, any TV programmes in the cozy genre etc.. It is also the place where I will be sharing what I'm writing, price drops but most of all letting readers know about FREE ARCs that will be available. Join me here:

Catherine's Cozy Corner

Catherine

Printed in Great Britain
by Amazon